Bad dogs, bad men, and bad luck.

Nothing stands in the way of revenge, romance, and rediscovery for the women in these stories, who make the most of second chances.

Whether coming to terms with lost love, or facing real and imagined demons on an amusement park ride, these women do what it takes to survive ... and then some. Stick with them through sunny days, shifting sands, stormy skies, and starry nights as they learn about life and love at the beach.

Award-winning writer Nancy Powichroski Sherman strikes just the right chord in this entertaining selection of stories, all set in towns along the shores of Delaware, Maryland, and New Jersey. Smile with recognition as characters in the stories run into the surf in Rehoboth Beach, ride the ferry from Lewes to Cape May, barhop in Dewey, sip lattes in Bethany Beach, stroll on the boardwalk in Ocean City, and visit the Wildwood amusement pier.

Sandy Shorts

Beach stories set in and around
Bethany, Cape May, Lewes, Rehoboth,
Ocean City, and Wildwood

By Nancy Powichroski Sherman

Cat & Mouse Press
Lewes, DE 19958
www.catandmousepress.com

ISBN-13: 978-0-9860597-1-1
ISBN-10: 0986059714

Cover illustration: Patti Shreeve
Cover design: It's a Snap Design
Dingbats: WC Fetish and WC Sold Out by WC Fonts; Nymphette by Lauren Thompson
Author photo: Carolyn Watson Photography

"Why You Trashed Vera Wang" was previously published in *The Beach House*, Cat & Mouse Press, 2013.

"The Gypsy Heart" was originally published in *Delaware Beach Life* magazine, April 2011.

"Letting Go" is a new telling of the story "The Sound of a Tree Falling," which was first published in *Delaware Beach Life* magazine, March/April 2007, as the fiction winner of the Rehoboth Beach Writers' Guild writing contest.

This collection of short stories is dedicated to:

My husband Matthew

Have I told you lately...?

In memoriam for:

My strongest cheerleader, my cousin Michael Powichroski
(August 16, 1951–August 16, 2010)

Thank you, cousin, for giving me stars that laugh.

Acknowledgments

I would like to thank Nancy Day Sakaduski, as both the editor and publisher, for creating a nurturing environment for the development and revision of these stories. Her editorial comments and suggestions were always honest yet supportive. Most of all, she was enthusiastic about publishing my first collection.

I would like to acknowledge both Maribeth Fischer and Linda Chambers for their inspiration and friendship. I have learned much from these two talented writers.

I would also like to express my appreciation to the Rehoboth Beach Writers' Guild for the opportunities to flex my creativity muscles and for the friendships that the guild fosters.

Finally, I would like to thank Browseabout Books for their support of the local writing community.

Table of Contents

Sunny
Days

The Lewes Ferry, a Five-pound Dog, and Romance

There were two things that had the power to make Maddie sick. One was being in a boat, and the other was being around pet dander. Yet, at this moment, she was driving onto the Cape May-Lewes ferry with a yapping dog in a small plastic carrier on the passenger seat. She hoped that the massive amount of Benadryl she'd taken earlier would cover both issues, but she wasn't convinced.

The ferry crewmember waved her into the right lane of the center section of the boat, behind a massive tour bus. Great view, she thought, though she had no intention of remaining in the car during the bay crossing. Her stomach preferred a clear sight-line to the horizon. The sooner she could escape the claustrophobia of this tightly packed parking area and be able to look out over the bay, the better. The stairs to the upper floors were just ten feet away, and she was anxious to claim a seat in the air-conditioned lounge. She reached for the dog carrier with one hand and began to open the driver's-side door with the other.

A loud air horn reverberated through the enclosed space and instinctively she yanked the door closed, just in time to avert having her door removed by an 18-wheeler that had been directed to the spot next to hers. The noise of the horn startled the dog into silence, which was a relief after all the barking she'd had to endure since picking up the dog at the Royal Beauties of Delmarva Kennels. In the quiet of the car, she could hear her heart pounding from the shock of almost losing a car door, and maybe even an arm, to the giant truck.

This day had "Excedrin" written all over it! She wondered if Excedrin and Benadryl were compatible, or if taking them together would result in her breaking out in horrible red splotches or going comatose and dying. Maddie would freely admit that she was a bit of a hypochondriac.

Why did I accept this contract? she asked herself. When she opened her business, Maddie's Messenger Service, her intention was to make local deliveries on land; she had not expected to be hired for an over-the-Delaware-Bay delivery to the southern Jersey shore, nor had she anticipated that the delivery would be a living thing, a dog, an allergen on four legs. So why *had* she accepted this delivery? Because, despite her allergies to dander and her tendency toward motion sickness, she needed the money, especially this month. Someone had sideswiped her car on Coastal Highway, rendering both passenger-side doors unusable. She needed to get her car repaired soon because loading and unloading everything from one side of the car was a real pain. The repair estimate was way more than she had expected, and her credit cards were already maxed out from the startup costs for her business. When she started her own company, she had anticipated financial security, but she quickly discovered that running her own business wasn't as lucrative as it had been described in the seminars from her Women Mean Business group. For this particular delivery, Royal Beauties of Delmarva Kennels was paying her more for transporting one of its dogs to a new owner in Cape May than she would earn by delivering a week's worth of local documents.

Traumatized by the blaring horn of the truck and the slam of the car door, the dog had disappeared to the back of its carrier. Though Maddie was certainly not a dog lover, she felt a bit sorry for it. "Okay, whatever-your-name-is," she said to the dog. "Let's get out of here." She again lifted the carrier and opened her door.

Thud! The truck was parked too close to her car for the door to open all the way. Fortunately, she knew that she was thin enough to squeeze sideways out of the car. She'd done it plenty of times in the Walmart parking lot during the summer season. After she shimmied out, she reached back into the car, grabbed the dog carrier, and then, another thud! The carrier was too big to pass through the limited opening of the door.

Damn, she thought, aggravated by the truck driver's inconsideration. She looked up at the writing on the cab of the truck: "Cape May Restaurant Supply."

"Hey!" she yelled, slamming her fist against the side of the truck. "Cape May Restaurant Supply! You've got to move over. You've blocked my door."

No response.

Now her temper was boiling. She climbed up on the step to the truck's passenger door. "Hey!"

No one was there. The driver had already exited and was probably enjoying coffee in the lounge, which was what Maddie wished she were doing. Some people drink coffee to stay awake, but Maddie drank coffee to calm down. She considered searching the ferry for an idiot with a Cape May Restaurant Supply logo on his shirt, and insisting that he jockey his rig a bit to give her room, but the reality of the situation stopped this thought. Already, other vehicles were parked behind both her car and the truck. Like some gigantic plastic slide puzzle minus its empty space, this was unsolvable.

If only the weather were colder, she could leave the crated dog inside the locked car and, unburdened, enjoy the bay crossing in the lounge upstairs. She could focus on watching the horizon from the lounge windows and avoid motion sickness. But with this summer heat, she couldn't choose that option. She had seen the public service announcements about the dangers to pets left in locked cars in the summer heat, and it was her duty to deliver a perfectly healthy dog to its new owner. With no other choice, she had to take the dog, minus its carrier, with her.

She reached over, opened the carrier door, and waited. The small, almost-hairless, brown dog with long white hair on its neck and ankles was huddled against the back wall of its enclosure, unwilling to exit. This was the first time Maddie had taken a good look at the dog she was delivering to Cape May. It looked like a Clydesdale horse, but was as tiny as a Chihuahua. "What breed are you?" she wondered aloud.

She looked at the dog's documents. "Chinese Crested. Chinese Crested what? You look more like the My Little Pony toy I had when I was a kid, except that you're not pink and purple." She peered into the carrier again. The dog remained against the back wall. "Look, I don't want to be with you either, but we have no choice. I'm being paid to take you to your new home in Cape May. Trust me that I wouldn't be within a yard of you if I didn't need the money so much."

Maddie had no experience with dogs, having grown up with so many allergies. She had no idea of how to get a dog out of a carrier when it didn't want to leave. She did know, however, that reaching into an enclosure in an effort to remove a cornered animal is never a good idea; she'd seen enough reality TV to convince her of that.

Call the dog, Maddie guessed. She checked the delivery documents again, this time for a name, but what she found was more like a regal title: "Royal Beauties of Delmarva Carnival Kewpie Doll Supreme." Wow. She couldn't believe that the dog would answer to all those names, but she tried anyway. "Come, Royal Beauties of Delmarva Carnival Kewpie Doll Supreme," she called, snapping her fingers as though that might add force to the command. The dog responded with a momentary head turn. Maddie couldn't decide whether the dog had responded to its name or simply reacted to the snapping fingers.

"Look," she said to the dog, as though bargaining with a human being, "I'm not going to call you that whole fancy name. It's ridiculous! I'll just call you … Little Pony. It's less embarrassing." She remembered her own teasing in high school French class when her classmates heard that her real name was Madeleine. "Like those French cookies, *those* Madeleines?" one of them had asked, and from that day on, they called her Cookie Monster. And the French teacher didn't stop them as long as they said it in French: "Monstre de gâteau." She had hated that, especially since "gateau" didn't just mean cookie; it also meant cake. Not a tiny cookie, but a full-sized cake. And she had been overweight in high school. Back then, if she'd been in this truck vs. car situation, she'd have been unable to squeeze through and would have been stuck inside the car for the entire Delaware Bay crossing.

Cookies. Maddie's stomach growled. Food. Of course! Maybe the dog is hungry, too. Quickly, she searched the bag that the kennel owner had included with the delivery instructions. Maybe there would be some Milk Bones or Beggin' Strips or any of those doggie things she'd seen on television commercials. But there weren't any snacks to be found. Just a small bag of dry dog food. "So that's why you're so skinny. You're on a diet!" she said. The dog food's name, Taste of the Wild, seemed a bit extreme for this small, cowering animal, but when she opened the bag, the dog came to the front of the carrier with its nose sniffing the air. "Oh, you like this, huh?"

Maddie held a handful of the food just beyond the carrier to entice the odd little dog onto the car console where she could grab it and attach a leash to its collar. "Gotcha!"

Surprisingly, the dog didn't react to the leash. It was too busy nosing the bag for more food. So that's how to get your attention, Maddie realized. *Lesson one: Dogs are like most of my friends—they respond best to food.* She dropped a handful into the fanny pack she wore; then, she lifted the dog into her arms and out of the car.

As she carried the dog up the narrow metal steps of the ferry, Little Pony vigorously squirmed in her arms. "Knock it off," Maddie warned the dog, but the struggle continued. At the top of the stairs, it jumped from her arms. Fortunately, Maddie had held tightly to the end of the leash, so the dog didn't escape, but it pulled to the left and under another outdoor staircase. "Whoa!" she commanded, too late, as the dog managed to wrap its leash around the railing of the staircase until it was tangled like Christmas lights in a storage container.

As Maddie knelt down to untangle the mess, the dog squatted and peed on the metal deck, causing Maddie to jump to her feet and let go of the leash. "Omigod, omigod," Maddie repeated over and over, looking around desperately and foolishly for paper towels or napkins or a discarded item of clothing, preferably one with "Cape May Restaurant Supply" embroidered on it. She glanced around to see if anyone had witnessed what had happened. No one. What a relief, she thought. As expected, everyone had rushed to the lounge area to snag a seat while Maddie had been struggling to get herself and the dog out of the car. No witness, no crime, she decided.

When she turned back to the staircase, the dog was gone. Panic time! A tiny dog like that could slip into any small place, or worse, it could fall through the railing slats and drown in the bay! "Damn, damn, damn!" Maddie rushed past the staircase calling, "Here, doggie, doggie, doggie," until she realized how stupid she sounded. "Here, Little Pony!" That didn't sound much better.

At the corner ahead, she saw the handle end of the leash. She slammed her foot on it and felt immediate relief as a tug on the other end proved that Little Pony was still attached. Keeping her foot firmly in place, Maggie reached down to grab the leash. Wet. Yuck! She didn't need to smell the leash to know that the dog had pulled it through the urine puddle. "I hate you, Cape

May Restaurant Supply! This is all your fault."

She scooped up the little dog and rushed through the door to the nearest restroom. Setting the dog in a sink, she slipped off the leash, cleaned it in soapy water, and reconnected it to the dog's collar. "Peeing on your leash is not going to make it go away. You're going to stick with me, and if that takes a wet leash, then so be it."

A high-pitched giggle was followed by, "Mommy, that lady said a bad word."

When Maddie saw that the child was pointing at her, she had to think for a minute to figure out what bad word she had said. She knew that she wasn't aggravated enough to have dropped the f-bomb. "I only said *peeing*," she explained to the mother, who gave her a look of disapproval and quickly pulled her daughter out of the restroom.

Maddie completed a thorough hand washing—thorough on the level of a surgeon scrubbing before an operation—and then picked up Little Pony and followed the hallway to the lounge. As she had guessed, the place was packed. She scanned the room, half-wishing that she'd see the guy from Cape May Restaurant Supply so she could guilt him into giving her his seat, since he was the reason that she hadn't gotten here early enough to claim her own. But she didn't see an overweight, baseball-capped, bearded moron with a greasy T-shirt and camouflage pants. Of course that was only her idea of what the jerk might look like. Her mental picture of a truck driver was colored by the stereotypes she'd seen in TV shows. No sign of a guy fitting that description.

It appeared that every seat was taken and every table was filled. Great. She wished that the three businessmen at a nearby table would be chivalrous and offer her the remaining seat, but she knew that wouldn't happen. Chivalry was dead. Feminism had killed it. She had to remind herself that feminism was a good thing and worth the loss of doors being held open and seats being offered. Feminism had gotten her a great job, right out of college, at Willoughby Wealth Management Consulting, one of the best agencies on the East Coast. Oh, that's right, she thought, the firm where the only female consultant—me—was the first to be tossed aside during downsizing. The only positive was that it spurred her to apply for and receive a loan to open her delivery company, though none of her clients knew that she was the only employee.

The little dog was much calmer now, and Maddie had learned something else: *Lesson two: Dogs let you know when they need to pee.* She'd have to focus more on Little Pony's body language to avoid another potentially embarrassing mishap, and as the dog tried to reach the flap to her fanny pack, Maddie was reminded of Lesson One, that a happy dog is one with food in its mouth. She reached in and brought out a few pieces of food for the dog to nibble.

Maddie needed sustenance herself and walked into the food court to get some much-needed coffee, and maybe a Danish if she was willing to be off her weight-loss plan. On any ferry trip across the Delaware Bay, she knew that getting coffee into a cup could be a difficult task, even with both hands free, but trying to do it while holding a squirming five-pound dog made the task almost impossible. Maddie tucked the dog under one arm, leaned her hip against the counter, and held her hand against the coffee machine, watching the hot liquid pour into the paper cup until it was full. She exhaled as she moved the cup to the side of the counter where the lids were stacked. Coffee sloshed around the edge of the cup as she pushed a lid into place. Then, she grabbed a wrapped pastry, telling herself that she had earned it, and balanced it on top of the coffee cup. She felt like a circus performer attempting a dangerous balancing act, keeping the pastry centered on the cup while maintaining control over a squirming dog, remaining steady despite the occasional shift of the ferry boat, and avoiding obstacles like the ice cream freezer and the small children who were racing toward it.

Victory! She made it to the cashier without dropping food, drink, or dog. With her hands and arms full, she asked the cashier to remove the required five dollars from her fanny pack. During the effort to locate the money, the cashier knocked some dog food to the floor, and Little Pony leapt from Maddie's arm to chomp down the two or three pieces within reach. Wrapping the handle of the leash around her wrist, Maddie quickly paid for her food and drink, then lifted the dog into her arms and restarted her search for any place where she could sit and eat.

She walked up and down the lounge but couldn't find an empty table or available seat anywhere, and her arms were cramping from holding the dog and balancing the pastry on the coffee cup. She remembered a friend from college who always chanted, "Saint Joan of Arc, help me find a place to park," when searching for a parking spot on Second Street in downtown Lewes during the summer season. At this moment, Maddie was willing to try anything, so she repeated it in her head like a mantra, *Saint Joan of Arc, help me find a place to park*, hoping that she wasn't being sacrilegious, *Saint Joan of Arc, help me find a place to park*, hoping that her repeating this saying over and over wouldn't result in the ferry sinking, *Saint Joan of Arc, help me find a place to park*. Just then, a man who had been single-handedly holding hostage a four-seat table while he read a newspaper, stood up, stretched, took out a pack of cigarettes, and left the lounge to find the smoking area of the boat. Maddie rushed to the table, claimed it with her coffee cup/pastry sculpture, and plopped onto the soft cushion of one of the chairs. She pulled another chair close by and put the pooch there, wrapping the leash around the chair back and thus freeing her own hands so she could eat her mini-breakfast.

She sipped the warm caramel mocha coffee. It was all the more delicious after what she'd been through to get it. The pastry, with its thick white icing glistening under the cellophane wrap, promised the same satisfaction. As she started opening the package, a man in a blue shirt approached. Her first thought was that this must be the truck driver. Maybe he's coming to apologize, now that he realizes the trouble he caused me, she thought. But the label on the front of the shirt indicated that the man was a crewmember of the ferry. Reality check, she said to herself. There's no way that truck driver gave me a thought.

"I'm sorry, miss," the crewmember said, "but pets are not allowed in the lounge unless they're inside a pet carrier."

"Well, this one would be inside a carrier if one of your staff hadn't put a giant tractor-trailer up against my car, preventing me from opening my door far enough," she snapped at him.

The crewmember furrowed his brow. "Your car has doors on both sides, right?"

She rolled her eyes. "The other side is damaged; the doors don't open."

"I'm sorry to hear that, miss, but the rules about pets are not negotiable. You'll have to take your dog to the outside deck and eat at one of the outside tables like the other pet owners."

No! Maddie could have exploded. She could have cursed. She could have cried. Instead, she exhaled every bit of air from her lungs, like a boxer that has just been delivered the end-of-the-match punch. She shoved the pastry into the pocket of her shirt, picked up the dog and her coffee, and said, directing her comments to the waiting crewmember and anyone else in the vicinity, "Well, Royal Beauties of Delmarva Carnival Kewpie Doll Supreme, it seems that no one here has any idea how important you are or they'd be scurrying to arrange a proper stateroom for you. Instead, you're being sent to steerage." Maddie could be fairly dramatic when a situation like this called for it.

She wasn't surprised that the outdoor benches were mostly empty. Why would anyone choose to remain outdoors on this hot and sticky morning? Briefly exploring the deck, she found two distinct areas: a section of smokers and a section of travelers with pets on leashes. Despite her frustration at not being able to eat her breakfast in the lounge, Maddie found humor in that moment. *Lesson Three: Dogs don't smoke.* The thought made her laugh, and laughter was just what she needed.

She walked toward the group of other travelers with pets and was glad to see some empty benches among them. At that moment, Royal Beauties of Delmarva Carnival Kewpie Doll Supreme again jumped from her arms. Apparently unaware of its diminutive size, the dog forsook its earlier fearful stance, and took on the role of alpha dog, barking in high-pitched tones at all the other dogs. They seemed a bit surprised at this sudden aggressiveness from what must have looked like a chew-toy to them. Maddie scooped the yapping dog into her arms, spilling a bit of her coffee as it splashed from the plastic lid, and offered a hasty apology to the other pet owners. Then, she fled to the top deck, hoping to find a seat there.

She was relieved to find a seating area that had been rejected by everyone else for its lack of shade. "This will have to do," she said to the dog, "thanks to you!" She tied the dog's leash through the handle of the first bench, burning the palm of her hand a bit on its sun-baked metal. "Maybe they should have named you 'Cujo,' like the vicious dog in the Stephen King story." Finally able to settle in, Maddie sipped her coffee and took a first delicious bite of the pastry. Relax, she thought, and she almost succeeded, but just then her canine companion whimpered.

"What now?" Maddie asked.

The dog gave her the sad eyes look.

"Hungry?" she asked. Maddie took out a few pieces of the dog food and laid them in front of the dog, but Little Pony ignored what had earlier been a treat and instead stared at the pastry in her hand.

"You've got to be kidding me!" she shouted to the sky. "Am I being punked down here?" She tore off a piece of the pastry and offered it to the dog. The whole morsel disappeared in one gulp. "Of course, you're going to like *my* food." And until the pastry was gone, Maddie gave the dog one piece of pastry for every two that she herself ate. It left Maddie hungry, but at least the dog was being well-behaved.

Her own stomach felt a bit queasy. Though the water was not choppy, Maddie still felt its effects. She glanced at her watch. Another forty-five minutes until she'd be in Cape May, where she would complete her delivery job and then enjoy a real meal in one of the town's wonderful restaurants. Her upset stomach reminded her of her last boat trip to Cape May, a date with a guy who owned a classy 24-foot Bayliner. The trip over to the Harbor View Restaurant was tolerable, and she had enjoyed a delicious crab cake sandwich and some oysters, but on the trip back, seasickness won. The crab cake and oysters didn't stay down, and she had returned to Delaware with her head over the side of her date's boat. He never asked her out again, and she knew that he had spread the story all over Rehoboth, Lewes, and Dewey, because she was never asked out again by anyone who owned a boat, or a jet ski, or a surfboard, or a skim board, or any other means of water transportation.

Suddenly, the dog started making a strange sound, and when Maddie looked down, she saw that the dog was throwing up. She put her hands over her face in frustration. "Why can't you be a pile of documents that I'm delivering and not a dog that barks and pees and pukes?" She hoped that when she looked again, she'd find that it was only her imagination and there was no mess to clean up. No such luck. "It wasn't enough that you peed under the staircase; now you're puking on the deck."

"Poor thing," a male voice said. "You're going to be okay."

Maddie startled with the realization that she was not alone. As she began to respond to the sympathy she fully felt she deserved, the guy knelt beside the dog and wiped its mouth with a faded blue bandana. Apparently, the only sympathy to be had was for the stupid dog. On the positive side, the guy was soap-opera hunky. His long, sun-bleached hair rested against the collar of his tight polo shirt, and his navy hiker shorts stretched tightly against muscular legs. When he looked up at Maddie, she saw beautiful green eyes and a handsome tanned face.

"Hi," was all that Maddie could say.

"You've got a beautiful Chinese Crested here. What's its name?" he asked.

Wow. He knew the dog's breed. "Royal Beauties of Delmarva Carnival Kewpie Doll Supreme," she answered, like a well-rehearsed line. "I'm delivering it to the new owner in Cape May."

His face lit up. "Oh, you're a dog breeder."

From his enthusiasm, Maddie decided that being a dog breeder must be a good thing, and it was definitely better than being a delivery girl. "Mmmhmm," she mumbled, and nodded, willing to be whatever would keep the conversation going, although she'd prefer a change of topic since she had so little knowledge of dogs.

"Do you have any more from this litter for sale?" he asked. "I have a friend in New York who would love one of these. Cresteds are the perfect size for city living." Then, he shook his head. "But why am I telling you this? You're the breeder; you know all about it."

Oh, no. He's serious about this dog stuff. "Of course," Maddie said. All about it.

"Has the dog been given a house name yet?" he asked.

House name? She had no idea what that meant. House name couldn't mean the name of the kennel; she'd already told him that. Maybe it meant whatever the dog was called around the house. "Little Pony," she answered, hoping that it would sound like a reasonable answer.

"Perfect name!" The guy accepted what she'd said and scratched the dog just above its tail, an action that the dog seemed to enjoy. Who wouldn't like being touched by this gorgeous man?

Gazing at him, Maddie did what she always did when she saw a cute guy; she fantasized about living with him in a cottage on the bay. But in this dream, they were sitting together with their Little Pony beside them on a porch swing. It was the one concession to her standard dream. As in all her fantasies, they would see each sunset like this, sipping a fine riesling or feeding each other sweet midnight-blue glenora grapes and slices of brie. She pictured them dressed in summer gauze, her in a flowing dress, and him in billowy slacks that tied at the waist. He would be shirtless, of course, like a guy on the front cover of a romance novel.

She imagined him dressed that way as she watched him rubbing the dog's back, "Feeling better, Little Pony?" he asked the dog.

Hearing the name spoken by someone other than herself pulled Maddie back to the real world and the awareness that Little Pony was her own invention and not the dog's real name. She panicked and blurted, "Actually, that's just a name that I call her. She's really Royal Carnival Supreme Kewpie Doll, you know," she said, mixing up the order of the dog's official name, but only realizing this after the words rushed from her mouth. "I mean," she slowly repeated, "Royal Beauties of Delmarva Carnival Kewpie Doll Supreme. It's just too long for a name, you know."

"I understand. I have a poodle, and she came with an AKC name already registered—High Mountains Sweet Blossoms Petals of Spring." He pointed his finger toward his mouth in a gagging motion. "Her house name is Petals, and I can't wait to get home and see her. I've been away for three weeks on business, and she's been staying with a friend of mine."

A friend? Maddie imagined a bikini-clad sex-goddess with big boobs waiting at the dock for him with a well-manicured poodle whose diamond-studded collar would match the tennis bracelet on the woman's arm. The woman would have a perfect smile and perfect teeth and be the perfect partner for this perfect guy who was so obviously out of Maddie's league. She could even see the two of them and their big poodle on her dream deck, sipping her wine and feeding each other her cheese and grapes.

Her dream popped like a cartoon balloon stabbed with a pin as she realized that he was still talking to her and that she hadn't been listening. "... and I really miss that little girl," he was saying.

Little girl? Does he mean the bikini woman, or did he say he has a child and I missed that? Maddie wished she had stayed focused.

"Consequently," he continued, "I've been petting every dog I've seen during these weeks away from home, especially poodles. That's why I was sitting with the dog people on the side deck."

"Oh, yes, the side deck," Maddie said, pulling herself together. "The place where Cujo here wanted to challenge every dog on the boat."

The guy laughed at the idea of the little Crested being a savage attack dog. "When I saw Little Pony in action back there, I thought, 'That dog's got spunk, as well as a very pretty owner.' So, I had to meet you."

So maybe there wasn't another woman waiting on the Cape May shore. Maddie tried hard to not blush, but she was sure that the heat on her face was not from the sun. Their eyes connected for a moment, and her smile matched his. Then, the dog stole attention again by rolling over on its back and waving its paws in the air, breaking the silent connection between Maddie and this guy she'd like to sit with on a porch swing with that riesling and brie.

"Someone wants a belly rub," the guy said, lifting the dog into his arms.

Yeah, I want a belly rub, Maddie thought, trying to hold back a naughty smile.

Her dream guy sat next to her with the dog in his arms. "It must be tough to let go of each litter."

Another reference to her being a dog breeder. "Of course," she responded, afraid to admit her lie and wreck everything, even though it was more about the fantasy than about any possible real future with a guy she just met on the ferry ride to Cape May. She carried an I'm-not-worthy feeling from her high school days as the overweight Cookie Monster.

Then, her handsome guy sneezed. And sneezed again. And when he sneezed a third time, he handed the dog to her. "Allergies. I guess I was near too much pet dander today. There was a woman downstairs brushing her golden retriever, and I suppose it wasn't a good idea for me to be hanging around during that."

This gorgeous man was allergic to dander. She had something in common with him, but she miraculously stopped herself from saying this as she realized how ridiculous it would be for her to be a dog breeder who was allergic to dogs. Still, thrilled at how this little dog had brought this sexy guy to her, Maddie hugged Little Pony and, in return, the dog licked her face. Immediately, Maddie sneezed and sneezed and sneezed and sneezed until she finally put the dog down on the deck and dug in her fanny pack for a tissue.

He smiled. "You run a kennel and are allergic to dogs? How do you cope with that?"

Her sneezing continued, much to Maddie's embarrassment. She expected that the Benadryl had run its course, and letting the dog get near her face had been a stupid mistake. As stupid as this charade she'd been playing. "I don't actually run a kennel. I'm sorry. I got caught up in the story, but it's not true. I'm just a delivery girl (sneeze) that the kennel hired to deliver Royal Beauties of (sneeze) Delmarva Carnival Kewpie Doll Supreme to the buyer. I don't even know much about dogs, though I admit that I've learned a few things from this one today (sneeze, sneeze)." She sniffled, then dabbed her nose. "I've really gotten to like this little dog. I kinda wish that I could have a dog of my own, but it wouldn't work out with my allergies."

"Sure you could have a dog," he said. "I have a one, remember? Petals? You just have to pick a breed with fur rather than hair. That's why I have a poodle. No dander." He pulled out his iPhone to show her a photograph of a curly white dog, and she was relieved that he didn't seem bothered by her little lies. "This is Petals. You'd like her. Sweet disposition, very loving." His smile sent warmth down her body that had nothing to do with the heat of this sunny day. "You'll have to meet her."

"I'd like to," Maddie said, hoping for the chance to have her fantasy come true, or at least to spend a little more time with this guy. And if it meant meeting another dog, then so be it. "When?" she asked, not willing to let this become just one of those keep-in-touch moments that never come to fruition.

"Today," he said with a determination in his voice that made Maddie hopeful that he was thinking the same thing. "After you deliver this cute little Crested to the new owner, meet me at the Rusty Nail. It's on the beachfront in Cape May; you can't miss it. The food is great, they have an outdoor dining area that is dog friendly, and they even have a menu for dogs. I'll pick up Petals, and we'll meet you there," he said, handing her a business card from his wallet.

"Ryan Alexander," she read from the card. "Owner and Operator, Cape May Restaurant Supply." It seemed impossible, but sure enough, this was her truck driver. The image of the beer-bellied truck driver evaporated. It took her a moment to recover from the shocking realization. "Cape May Restaurant Supply," she repeated.

"Family business," he explained. "And you?"

"Maddie." She fished out one of her own business cards. "Maddie's Messenger Service," she said. "Need anything delivered?"

"You," he said with a wink.

And she knew, deep in her heart, or at least in her imagination, that she could overcome seasickness for this guy, and that she could be a dog lover, or at least a dander-free-dog lover, as long as the reward was a chance to sip wine and eat grapes with him at sunset and end up in his arms.

The Two-to-One Rule

You'd been cautiously looking forward to this week at Rehoboth Beach with Deanna and Kira, a vacation that had been planned over hot chocolate from the vending machine at work one day last February when an unpredicted snowstorm brought everyone together. It would be the first trip for the three of you together. Three? Haunting memories of ninth grade crash through your mind, memories of a BFF tragedy when your friend-since-birth, Shauna, was lured away onto the cheerleading squad and into its social world, leaving you to wander through the first semester of high school in search of a lunch table. Push aside the pain of that teenaged abandonment, and replay the more recent hot chocolate fiasco. When Deanna sighed, "Let's go to the beach," you should have said, "The *two* of us at Rehoboth again? Great idea," before Kira had the opportunity to squeal, "Ooh, count me in." Now you think of *He who hesitates is lost*, and regret having taken a sip of tongue-burning hot chocolate at that crucial moment. The old adage, *Two's company, three's a crowd*, should have sent a bright red flare into the blizzard-white sky that day, but it obviously didn't, because Deanna shocked you with her answer of "Sure. Why not?" Really? Earlier that week, she had called Kira a social climber with the fashion sense of a hoochie-momma and the vocabulary of a twelve-year-old. When you confronted Deanna during happy hour at the Owl Bar about the threesome vacation, she swore that she was just playing with

Kira the way a spider plays with a fly and that she intended to "find a reason" to un-invite her in a few weeks.

A few weeks disappeared into months. Fridays became the three of you sitting at the Owl, like characters from *Sex and the City*. Kira started dressing better, and you assumed that Deanna was giving her private fashion advice. But when Kira spoke, her vocabulary and grammar still made you cringe. As the saying goes, *It's better to be thought a fool, than to open your mouth and remove all doubt.* Yet, she was friendly to you, and you started to feel badly about your criticisms of her. She had probably not been given the educational advantages you had. You had to remind yourself that she's a secretary in the pool, not an administrative assistant like you and Deanna.

But then small disagreements surfaced between you and your best friend, and you became suspicious that Kira was the instigator. It hurt you to think that another BFF relationship was in danger and that Deanna, who'd been your best friend since sharing a dorm room in college, might be inching away from you and moving closer to this other girl. You want to remind her of Benjamin Franklin's words, *Be slow in choosing a friend, slower still in changing*, but you know how much your famous quotations annoy her. It would be *like adding fuel to the fire.* (Okay, Deanna's right. You do overuse old sayings.) Make a resolution to keep these to yourself. If Deanna can't hear them, then they don't exist, right?

You did consider pulling out of the Rehoboth trip, but you feared that it would give Kira her chance to replace you. So, you decided to hold tight to your position, even though it meant pretending to be one of the Three Musketeers. *Easier said than done.* (Oops!)

Now you wonder if you made the right decision. You aren't sure whether it was coincidence or some ridiculous power game that clicked in two weeks before the vacation drive, but it seemed as though Deanna was purposely making strange suggestions of "fun things for us to do." While you looked at Deanna as though she were crazy, Kira eagerly agreed to every odd suggestion.

The worst of all these "fun" activities happened on the day before the three of you left Baltimore for the beach. Deanna proposed that you go together to a local spa to get Brazilian waxes. What?! When Kira practically jumped up and down like a kid on Christmas morning, it was useless for you to express your lack of enthusiasm for a torture you had so far avoided. Neither of them seemed the least bit concerned about exposing such a private area to a total stranger, licensed esthetician or not. But, regardless of your sensitivities, you were not going to walk away. The memory of that afternoon still makes you blush with embarrassment, but you carry your irritated skin as a badge of fealty.

Now, three days into the Rehoboth vacation, you're on the edge of mutiny. You have bungee-jumped in Ocean City, taken kayaking lessons in Fenwick Island, and had your hair braided in Rehoboth. Always Deanna's ideas. Always Kira's wholehearted agreement. The two-to-one rule is the mantra of this vacation, as Deanna's and Kira's votes win every time. You're grateful that Deanna hasn't suggested that you all get your heads shaved and have Kermit the Frog tattooed on your forehead! Kira would agree, and then what would you do?

Today's activity is finally something safe and welcome, something you actually want to do—shop the outlets. You wave a flyer from the *Delaware Coast Press* announcing a huge sale at the QVC outlet: eighty percent off clothing, sixty percent off shoes and accessories, even fifty percent off Birkenstocks, for goodness sake! However, Deanna doesn't receive the news with joy. She rolls her eyes and says, "Really, Bethie? My mom wears that stuff. Elastic waistbands on jeans! Decals and sequins on sweaters! I wouldn't be caught dead in anything they sell."

What? Deanna has been salivating over the cute little hoodie you wore last night when the three of you went barhopping. Funny how she doesn't remember that the hoodie is a QVC item you ordered online one day at work when the company had pizza sent in for everyone and you ate lunch at your desk rather than crowd into the conference room where the pizza boxes took up most of the space.

Kira jumps in with her two cents. "I certainly wouldn't set foot in a QVC outlet." She and Deanna fist-bump in agreement.

You almost burst out in laughter. Maybe Kira hadn't set foot in the outlet, but she most certainly watches QVC on television and orders items by phone. The necklace she's wearing is from the Kirks Folly collection, a designer that is part of the "QVC family." You purposely look at the necklace until you know that, dumb as she is, she finally understands your meaning. You could call her out on the Kirks Folly right here, right now, but you decide to save that for a later time. *Revenge is a dish best served cold.* (You didn't say it aloud. Why would you? That would defeat the whole purpose.)

Kira quickly adds, "Besides, Bethie, wouldn't you rather shop at the designer outlets?"

Only Deanna is allowed to call you Bethie. Feel the rebellion swell inside of you. Announce to Deanna, whose car is the transportation during this week in Rehoboth, that you'd like to be dropped off at the QVC outlet while she and Kira go to the Midway Outlet stores. "Yes," you tell her, "I am aware that I will be missing out on all your favorite designers: Michael Kors, Kate Spade, Coach, and yes, even Dooney & Bourke, for goodness sake." You saved her favorite for last just to watch the impact.

Deanna's lips tighten into a thin line. "They're your favorite designers, too, Bethie."

"Maybe," you say. "But I'll be at the QVC sale." Smile, but not a sarcastic smile. Keep it friendly and light. *Choose your battles wisely.* There's no sense in wrecking the rest of the vacation by starting a war that you can't win. The two-to-one rule has more power than you.

She gives you a "whatever," and returns an equally saccharine smile. You hope you haven't made a terrible mistake; you've just given Kira an afternoon alone with your best friend. But you think about the coral knit mini-dress you glimpsed on the QVC network while you were channel-surfing last week and how difficult it had been to keep your finger from dialing the customer service number on the screen. You consider how much that dress would have cost you at a department store. More importantly, you think about the eighty-percent discount waiting for you at the QVC outlet.

When they drop you off, there's a long line of women waiting to enter to the store. Make the most of it by saying, "Looks like this is the place to be."

Kira surprises you with, "Yeah, if you're forty."

"Nice necklace, Kira," you say. "Are you sure you don't want to join me?"

No answer, but a glance that practically dares you to comment on her necklace. Lucky for her, or maybe unlucky for her, you're saving that little secret for something bigger. *He who laughs last, laughs best.* (Okay, this quotation thing really has gotten out of hand.) Scan the line for women in their twenties, but don't see anyone fitting that age range. Come up with a smart response. "Obviously, the twenty-somethings like us were savvy enough to get here early so they wouldn't be stuck in line with the senior citizens."

Now you question your decision to choose this solitary outlet, attached only to carryout food eateries, over the larger collection of prime outlets at Midway, where Deanna and Kira are heading, but there's no way that you're going to admit this to them. It's like the time you ate a raw oyster at a boating party; you forced yourself to forget that this just-shucked oyster was still an uncooked living thing, and you swallowed that slimy gray blob as though you enjoyed it. Then you spent the rest of the night pouring strawberry daiquiris down your throat to get rid of the taste and ended the evening drunk and nauseated.

"See you in a bit," you say as you exit the car. Walk proudly to the end of the customer line. Give a Miss America smile and wave as Deanna drives off with Kira replacing you in the front passenger seat. Don't let them see that you're worried this replacement is symbolic of her replacing you permanently.

You're glad they're gone when a horde of elderly women line up behind you, squawking like a flock of seagulls about the heat and humidity. This chorus of complainers makes a few seconds drag into minutes that feel like hours waiting in the line. The loudest one is droning on and on in a nasal monotone, "What's taking so long? Why aren't they letting us in more quickly? Didn't they plan for this? Don't they know how hot it is out here?" Her voice is like fingernails on a chalkboard. It brings back bad memories of Dr. Henrietta Coolidge, your statistics professor in college. Her voice was so irritating that you often cut class to avoid the sound of it. You tried to study on your own in the dorm. Of course, your dorm room wasn't much better, with all the chatting from Deanna, and you barely squeaked by with a B-minus. Panic grabs you. Could it actually *be* Dr. Coolidge standing behind you? Would she remember you? Would she know that you were one of the students who left the Ben Stein *Ferris Bueller's Day Off* button on her office corkboard? You turn and get a quick look; you're relieved to find a woman whose physical characteristics are nothing like Dr. C's.

Your cell phone signals a text message from Deanna: "Joke over? Ready 4 pickup?"

Type, "2BZ shopping deals. L8TR."

Be glad that she texted rather than phoned you. The sound of the traffic on Route 1 would have given away your lie.

After a large group of customers exit the store, the line moves forward and you are fortunate to get into the outlet. Smile, knowing that Miss Monotone didn't make the cut and is still waiting outside. Feel relief that you don't have to listen to her whining anymore.

Inside, the store is filled with aisles and aisles of clothing racks packed tightly, and in each aisle, customers are jammed together, bumping into one another, reaching over one another, and lifting items into the air and stacking them onto their armloads of possible purchases. You see designer names heading each rack, with size markers scattered throughout, and you work your way to the Denim & Company section, hoping to find some cropped pants to match your sweatshirt. You spot the blue-and-white striped fabric in the section marked "Medium." You get butterflies, believing that you have found the Holy Grail of match-ups. Before a lumpy woman in pink shorts and an awful polka-dot tank top can grab it, you lunge forward and score. *The early bird gets the worm!*

You're the winner in the game of sale shopping. You admire the cropped pants only long enough to realize that there is no way these pants are size medium. Read the label. 2X! Accept that the pink-shorts-woman can have these, and place them where you found them, making sure she sees this. She does. She practically mows you down to get to the hanger.

Find an assortment of sizes clumped in with the mediums and know that customers are purposely hiding large sizes in with the small ones, and small sizes in with the large ones, a well-known strategy for protecting a potential purchase for a later visit. Most of them never return, and in the meantime, other customers of that size walk right past them. Feel righteous anger crawl up your spine. Your search for treasure is going to be more daunting than you'd anticipated, but you absolutely must score at least one awesome piece of clothing, one absolutely spectacular item, to save face with Deanna and Kira. Somehow, in this sea of people and clothing, you must find the priceless pearl, or in this case, something that will look so incredible on you that both the other girls will be speechless. *Leave no stone unturned.* Or a better slogan for your treasure hunt: *All things come to he who waits.*

Plant yourself in what seems to be a rack of mostly cotton knits, armed with a battle plan: Ignore the size markers and examine everything. Slide hanger after hanger, giving each item the quick check. Reject any that are wrong size, wrong color, unknown designer, or aren't currently trending. Pile any sexy mediums on your left arm until the weight becomes too heavy; then glance around to find a dressing room. Spot it in a side corner of the store. Maneuver your way to that corner.

Despite some bumps and almost dropping your pile of knits, you reach the door to the dressing room. Like Christopher Columbus rejoicing upon reaching the new world, feel triumphant at finding no waiting line. Reach for the door, and discover the padlock on the latch. Stare at it for a moment. The heat must have you hallucinating. A padlock? Could this one be a storage closet? Read the sign again. "Dressing room." No doubt. But there can't be a padlock on the dressing room. Surely there has been some terrible mistake, some oversight in the store's preparations.

Look for a saleswoman and see one who is emptying a box of handbags and hanging them on wall hooks under a sixty-percent-off sign. Inform her that the dressing room is locked. Expect her to be shocked. "I know," she says without stopping her task. "We keep it locked during the big summer sale."

"Why?" you ask, confused.

She sighs. "Over the years, we have learned to keep the dressing rooms off-limits during this once-a-year summer sale. With so many customers on these sale days, there have been arguments among them about who's taking in too many clothes and who's taking too long to try them on. There were times when we thought we'd have to call the police before anyone got hurt. Then, there was the problem of customers leaving their rejects piled on the floor of the dressing room until the mirror inside was completely blocked by the mountain of clothes."

"Then how do I know if these tops fit?" you ask.

"Buy them, and bring back any that don't fit. You have thirty days for returns," she says to you. "Or, you can do what the regulars are doing." She points to a full-length mirror on the back wall. There, you see women in various stages of undress, trying on clothes in the open, not the least bit ashamed to show their dingy bras and saggy bellies.

After surviving the Brazilian wax, this is child's play. You join them and try each top, vying for your turn in front of the mirror. Half in, half out of a plunging black sleeveless tank, your cell chimes again.

"R U OK?" Deanna texts.

"Yes. In dress room," you lie, though this back aisle has become a group dressing room. "No time 2 type. Will call u." Hope that this top fits. You need to have something to prove that Deanna and Kira should have come here with you.

Each top fits. *Good.* Each top looks sexy. *Excellent.* And with the eighty-percent discount, all seven items will cost a total of thirty-five dollars! Assure yourself of what a deal this is, especially since the labels all contain the names of designers. Sure, none of them are Deanna's favorite designers, so none of them will impress her, but each top is so great on your body that it doesn't matter. Or does it? Not one of these will prove Deanna wrong; not one of these will silence Kira; not one of these will win the battle, and not one of these will get Deanna to step inside the QVC doors, even though she can't buy so much as a scarf for thirty-five dollars at one of her outlets.

Resigned to losing the challenge, look for the best path to the checkout line.

Then, you see it! Not the checkout line. Something a thousand times better. A grape leather Dooney & Bourke hobo handbag in the hand of the saleswoman who has been unpacking purses. She has just lifted it from the box and is reaching up to hang it under the sixty-percent discount sign. Leap toward it before it reaches the display hook, almost knocking the employee down. Hug the purse to your chest and apologize. This is the exact bag Deanna wants. It's also her favorite color, purple. And sixty percent off the QVC price of $279 makes it $111! Deanna will faint. You almost feel as though you could.

Excited and anxious to dangle this in front of Deanna and Kira, bump and crash through the aisles toward the checkout line. On arrival, gasp, not out-of-breath, but at the sight of how long the line is. At least twenty-five customers, all with arms full of clothing, shoes, scarves, and purses, are waiting for the register. No one has anything as great as the Dooney & Bourke, though. You get jealous stares from several of the women. One offers to buy it from you. You smile and decline, beaming with your treasure. *"Slow and steady wins the race,"* you say with pride. Your saying goes unappreciated.

As the line inches forward, you find yourself reaching out to items on the racks that border the checkout aisle, rejects that customers have plopped on the ends of racks rather than put back in the right sections. It's not that you really *need* a fuchsia sweater, but the color catches your eye and you need to touch the fabric and check the tag anyway. It's something to do to pass the time while waiting. You're not the only one doing this. The line in front of you seems choreographed with reach, lift, inspect, and return to the end of the rack, though occasionally an item gets added to someone's arm-pile. The sweater doesn't get added to yours.

Your cell phone dings with another text message from

Deanna. "Kira driving me nuts. Can i pick u up now?"

Type "not yet," and add a smiley face.

Kira has finally gotten to Deanna? It seems too sudden. There is no way that a few minutes could do damage that hadn't already taken place in the past few months. Then an idea hits you. Maybe Deanna never really liked Kira at all. Could she have carried on a spider-and-the-fly game all this time for no reason?

Consider giving away the grape Dooney & Bourke handbag. But first, take a cell phone photograph of the bag. Click a front view of the bag, a side view, and a shot of the inside fabric. Smile like the Grinch on Christmas day. Then take a selfie as you hold the bag in your arms. Plan to share this proof of your find with Deanna at a later serious discussion about the bond of friendship. "Too bad I had to put the bag back," you'd say to her, "but I couldn't put that on my credit card when I wasn't sure that we were friends anymore." Hold the purse out toward the end of the next rack, but quickly pull it back. You can't do it. No matter the hurt Deanna had caused you in the silly game with Kira. She was, and always will be, your friend. Remember: *He who plots to hurt others often hurts himself.* Maybe this adage is worth saying directly to Deanna next time you can have a private conversation.

Behind you, you hear a familiar drone. It's the Dr. Coolidge twin, complaining, "Why don't they have more cashiers? Why aren't they doing something about this wait? Why are they making us stand in line so long?"

Apparently, this woman only converses in questions. You wonder how her friends put up with her, and why she doesn't seem to recognize her annoying habit of rhetorical question after rhetorical question.

Just like you drop old sayings into every conversation.

The realization hits you so hard that you almost drop the purse and piles of fashionable tops from your arms. Acknowledge that you're probably just as annoying as this droner and that the

Dooney & Bourke handbag is compensation for your BFF putting up with you all these years.

Moments before you reach the cashier, you are shocked as Deanna bounds through the doors and rushes over to you. "Omigod," she says. "Never, ever, leave me alone with Kira again."

"I thought you two were the perfect partnership. You and Kira agree on everything. You were the two to my one," you remind her.

Deanna chews her lower lip like she has always done when caught doing something wrong. "My mistake. From now on, you and I have to stick together."

For the tiniest moment, you consider turning the game on her and letting her suffer just a bit for all she put you through, but the soft leather of the Dooney & Bourke reminds you of your pledge to this friendship. "Well, that depends. As long as you don't make me get any more Brazilian waxes or go bungee jumping, you can count on me."

Deanna takes a breath and says, "As you have often said, *To err is human, to forgive divine.*"

She got you. You smile, and toss out an adage of your own, "*Time heals all wounds.*"

Deanna holds out her pinky. "Friends?"

"Always." You look toward the door. "So where's Kira?" You hope that Deanna will say that she sent her home to Baltimore on the nearest Greyhound bus.

"She's waiting in the car." Then she adds, "Don't worry. I rolled the windows down a bit. The SPCA would be proud of me."

The dog reference is mean, but it gives you the opportunity to use one more adage. "You know, Deanna, *He that lies down with the dogs riseth with fleas.*"

She scratches her forearm. "Lesson learned." Then she gets

serious. "Bethie, I really am sorry. I put you through a lot, and honestly, I'm not proud of how I've treated Kira either. The game just got away from me." Then she notices the grape leather purse in your arms. "Oh!" Her face whitens. "The Dooney & Bourke store was out of that bag. I had to settle for an aqua satchel."

"How much?" you ask her.

She beams with the pride of scoring a bargain. "It was originally $398, but the fifteen-percent discount brought it down to $338."

Then you show her the tag on your purse. "And sixty percent off of that number," you say.

Deanna almost chokes on her gum.

"There's more," you tell her, pointing to the handbag wall. "You could have bought two Dooney & Bourkes here for the price you paid at the other outlet."

It takes less than five seconds for Deanna to spot the display. She races in that direction like an Olympian, jumping over small children, swinging around the ends of racks, knocking over a few shoppers in the way. You watch as she pulls down the entire row of handbags. No grape left. She holds all eight bags, maintaining temporary ownership until she can decide which to buy. Without her favorite color, she picks both an ivy one and a strawberry one and carries both to you.

"Which one?" she asks you, like in the old days at college when you shopped together for special events like homecoming.

You've always been a fan of green, so you say, "Definitely the ivy green one."

"If you're not going to buy that red purse, I'll take it," a nasal voice says. You almost gasp. It's the first time the Dr. C clone has spoken a complete thought without framing it into a question.

"Want it?" Deanna asks and hands it to the woman who finally shows that her face is capable of a smile.

As you step up to the cashier, you take Deanna's ivy purse and hand her the grape one. "It's your color, after all."

Deanna looks as tickled as a child with cotton candy. As she takes out her credit card for the purse, she says, "You know, Kira hates sushi."

"Really? So sushi tonight at the Cultured Pearl?" you ask.

She nods. "It's the two-to-one rule."

Rescued Love

Haley had quit so many things in her life that she'd lost count. Some things she quit when her body insisted, things like snowboarding and distance cycling. Some things she quit before they quit her, like passing the CPA exam or getting her pilot's license. And other things she claimed to give up when, in reality, she never actually had them in the first place, like wearing a size six dress or participating in the Exercise Like the Eskimos winter ocean plunge here in her hometown of Bethany Beach. Now, she wished she'd stuck with something so that life would still owe her a quit ticket and a chance to walk away from her current task—parenting a dog!

She looked down into the eyes of Bingo, all seven pounds of gray and white fur, with his innocent eyes that showed no acknowledgment of the puddle in the middle of the Chinese Fateh rug that had been passed down through three generations of Woodward women.

"Bad dog!" she said in her sternest voice, shaking her finger at him.

Its effect? Not what she expected. Bingo wagged his tail as though he'd done something wonderful, licked her finger, and gave her a big "love me" face.

Haley was at a loss as to what she should do. The dog had been with her for only two days, and so far, he had spilled his water bowl across the hand-scraped oak floor, torn and scattered her Sunday *New York Times*, and dropped half-eaten doggie treats throughout the house, like doggy bank deposits saved for a rainy day. All of these had been unpleasant, but now the rug! Staining this priceless rug was not acceptable. And what expensive or irreplaceable item would the dog go for next? Would Bingo decide to chew a leg of the antique mahogany bench in the foyer, or shred one of her Jimmy Choo shoes? Her new leopard ones that cost her close to $600? No, the dog would be sent packing before she'd let that happen. She never should have tried this pet ownership thing in the first place.

She grabbed her iPhone from its charger and started to hit a speed-dial button, but stopped. She couldn't quit this time. No, this time she had to succeed. It was a dare, and she refused to lose a dare, especially to her ex-boyfriend Brent, who had accused her of being self-centered and had challenged her to prove otherwise by taking in a rescue dog. *Rescue.* That word had seemed so uplifting at the time. The deal was that, if she successfully fostered a rescue dog for the whole summer, Brent would treat her to a September weekend in New York, where he would be her caddy while she spent hours in her favorite sport—shopping Fifth Avenue. An easy dare, she had thought. For years, she watched Brent, who was a volunteer at the Delaware SPCA, as he fostered dogs, sometimes two at once, and it looked so effortless. Give them food, take them for a walk, and follow them with a pooper-scooper (the only part of the project she wasn't keen on). And the dogs that Brent fostered were usually the tough, strong-willed breeds that no one else at the shelter could handle, like Rottweilers and Pit Bull Terriers, yet they were so gentle under his guidance. If Brent could turn guard dogs into family pets that were quickly adopted, then certainly Haley could survive this little four-legged puff of fur. Or so she thought. She put her cell phone into her back pocket just in case she changed her mind.

She carried Bingo into the kitchen, set him on a tall chair to keep him out of trouble, and rooted through the cleaning supplies in the cabinet under the sink: dishwashing detergents, scouring pads, two flashlights, bug spray, emergency candles, and assorted surface cleansers. Nothing for cleaning a rug. It was an I-could-have-had-a-V8, smack-in-the-head moment. Of course there weren't any rug cleaning products under the sink. She had never needed to remove a rug stain before now; she lived alone, and whenever she had parties, her office was off-limits to guests. Still, it would have been nice if the cleaning fairy had left something under the kitchen sink that might work.

She sighed. She had planned to spend today catching up on her fashion blog, "Haley's Must-Haves," and Photoshopping some images for the webpage. Instead, she had to act quickly to save the rug before Aunt Alice, matriarch of the Woodward family, found out about this incident; it could be enough to cost Haley her stewardship of the family heirloom.

Her aunt would never understand. Aunt Alice was a cat person. In her aunt's opinion, cats were sophisticated houseguests, while dogs were uncivilized interlopers.

"Dogs," her aunt would say, "interrupt your life. You must entertain them. Unlike cats, who are, by nature, self-sufficient. Give cats a dish of food, and they nibble it neatly, often politely leaving a bit behind like a well-mannered young lady. Dogs inhale the contents of the bowl, and then lick the emptiness as though expecting more to suddenly appear. Cats keep their business hidden in a litter box, while dogs relieve themselves anywhere and everywhere. No thank you! Cats are the only animals deserving of the title 'domesticated,' my dear." Aunt Alice kept a pure white Maine Coon cat named Alabaster, who paraded through her aunt's house as though she were a queen, and who apparently was planning to live to the age of Methuselah, just like her owner.

No time to think about Aunt Alice and her monstrous cat. Haley grabbed a handful of paper towels, rushed back to the rug, and blotted the dog pee until all that remained was a dark circle that could soon become a permanent stain. She pulled her iPhone from her pocket and, with the assistance of Siri, contacted a local rug cleaner for their advertised "expert Oriental rug service." After setting up an afternoon rug pickup, Haley could finally relax.

When she felt a lick on her bare foot, she realized that Bingo had managed to jump down from the tall kitchen chair where she had left him, despite the height from seat to floor, without breaking a leg, thank goodness. She could just imagine having to rush the dog to a vet and pay an exorbitant bill that, added to the cost of cleaning the Woodward heirloom rug, would postpone her purchase of that Michael Kors clutch bag she'd been admiring online for weeks. She was going to need to pay more attention to where she left the furry nuisance in the future. At least for now, that clutch bag was still within her reach.

If she were going to win the bet with Brent and get her shopping spree in New York, she realized that she needed to treat this dog ownership dare as a work project, complete with plans and calendar. She took a notebook from her desk and started a list of problems and potential solutions:

> A teething dog = a chew toy
> Inappropriate peeing indoors = doggie diapers
> Lack of discipline = find a trainer
> House not dog-proofed = purchase items to remedy this

There was a place on Garfield Parkway, a store called Cold Nose Warm Heart. It was the kind of pet boutique where they sold organic pet treats, clothing for dogs, and gifts for pet owners. The only reason Haley knew about it was that the store was situated in the heart of Bethany, not far from Bethany Beach Books, where she picked up her beach reads, and The Artful Bean, her favorite coffee spot. One time, she wandered into the pet store to buy a gift for her BFF Leslie's Beagle, a present to take to Beagle Bailey's Birthday Bash, and she was delighted that the proprietor let her bring her latte into the store. She remembered that he was a nice old guy with a European accent. The same flirty smile that helped her keep her latte that day would surely work its magic again and she could coax some advice from him on how to address all the dog problems on her list without Brent ever knowing.

Haley smiled. Already, what had seemed an impossible undertaking was looking possible. She scooped up Bingo, put him into an L.L. Bean canvas tote bag (the best she could do until she could find a classy doggy purse like the Louis Vuitton one she had seen in a photograph of Paris Hilton), and headed out the door, hoping for a one-stop treasure box of everything she needed, from toys to home protection.

Kazimierz, or Kaz as his friends called him, was the kind of man who never left the house without a dog biscuit or two in his pocket, who sent a check every month to the local shelter, and who didn't own a pet because he believed that one living being shouldn't own another living being, yet he was the proprietor of a pet store. Every day, he'd open a bag of biscuits and fill a jar of treats by the cash register to give to anyone who brought a dog into his store. He always placed the free treats strategically next to a small display of flyers about spaying and neutering, a cause he supported. Kaz observed how the dogs were being treated. He was always prepared to assist with any problems, and his cell phone contained the number for a rescue organization for nearly every breed. He had a pat on the head and words of comfort for any dog on a leash, and he bent down to say what the human being attached to the other end of the leash never heard. "Wy jesteście kochani." In his native Polish, it meant "You are loved."

Kaz propped open both doors to let the spring air swirl through the store and drive out the mustiness of the winter as he stocked the shelves for the quickly approaching tourist season. Already, summer visitors were down for the weekends and the sidewalk that led to the boardwalk was busy with walkers, cyclists, couples, and families, and though it wasn't warm enough for a dip in the ocean, the teenaged girls were already in their summer flip-flops and short-shorts.

"Kaz!" someone called out.

He turned as Brent, one of his best customers, entered the store holding tightly to the leash of a black Mastiff, and leading the dog quickly through the store entrance and away from the high squeals of some nearby children, who were reacting as if the dog were a monster. "Got any of those ginger treats?"

Kaz reached into a canister for a large biscuit. He held it lightly in his hand and offered it to the dog, who, despite its size, took the treat gently.

"I'm fostering this guy until we can be sure he has the good manners to fit in with a permanent family." Brent smiled. "I'm calling him 'Bear' for now since we couldn't find any identification on him when we picked him up wandering along the wooded area near Selbyville. We scanned him, hoping for an embedded ID chip. Nothing. Of course, no one in the area claimed him. We figure it was a drop-and-drive from someone who couldn't handle his size or couldn't afford to feed him anymore."

When the dog finished chomping down the treat, Kaz let the Mastiff sniff his hand, then he rubbed the dog's chest and whispered, "Dobry pies (good dog). Wy jesteście kochani."

The big dog licked Kaz's arm.

Brent smiled. "Hey, Kaz, he likes you. Maybe you'd take him as is, without my fostering him."

Kaz stood. "He's too big for a one-human home. He needs

kids and activity, not life with an old guy like me."

Brent grinned. "If Bear's too big, I might have a little guy for you. A Havanese puppy. Sad story. He belonged to an elderly woman in Fenwick Island who passed away suddenly, without a family or any legal instructions on what to do with her possessions. Apparently, her dog was considered one of those possessions, so the lawyer who was appointed to her case brought the dog to the SPCA. End of problem. Well, end of problem for the lawyer, but leaving a sweet little guy who needs a permanent home. Right now, I've got him in a temporary situation, staying with a friend of mine, but I know that won't last. So how about it? Ready to adopt?"

Kaz handed another biscuit to the Mastiff. Though his philosophy was against pet ownership, he was lonely. Maybe it was time for a companion. "Maybe," he said. "But only maybe."

On her way to the pet shop, Haley detoured into The Artful Bean for a skinny iced mocha. Gina, the barista behind the counter, showered Bingo with attention. "Where did you find such a precious puppy?"

Haley glowed with pride. Not quite the level of pride she would have had if she were carrying a Hermes leather satchel instead of a dog in a canvas tote bag, but pride nevertheless. "I rescued him," she bragged, reaching into her L.L. Bean tote to lift the dog into her arms. "Aren't you the best little puppy in the world?" Her tone wavered a bit when she noticed the tiny wet spot at the bottom of the tote. She kept her smile in place as she lowered Bingo back into the bag, all the while wondering how long she could keep up this pretense of being a doting pet owner. Could she survive long enough for her New York prize?

"If you ever need a dog sitter, call me," Gina said.

Haley made a mental note that, after winning the dare, she could pass off the dog to Gina. A win-win opportunity. "If I ever find that I can't keep Bingo, you'll be first in line to be the new doggy momma." As she turned to leave, Haley caught a glimpse of Brent outside the shop. Quickly, she turned her back, almost spilling her drink, and hoped that he hadn't seen her. She was not ready to face him; he knew her too well to believe her phony joy in dog ownership. When she glanced again toward the entrance, he was gone. Sneaking a closer look, she saw that Brent and a monstrous black beast were walking down Central Boulevard toward Coastal Highway. Good. She could safely slip into the pet store unnoticed.

It took less than a minute for Kaz to know that Bingo was the Havanese that Brent had told him about, and that the frazzled girl who carried the puppy in her large bag was Brent's friend, the one providing the temporary home. The girl had too many questions to be a foster parent for the SPCA. It gave Kaz the suspicion that there was more to this story than Brent had told him.

"So how many pets have you fostered?" he asked her.

"This is my first and last," she said, while lifting the puppy from her bag. "Any chance I could have some wet paper towels?"

Kaz provided the necessary towels, and the girl held out her dog to him. "And could you hold Bingo for me?"

As Kaz took the puppy, he watched the girl furiously wiping out the bottom of her tote. "He peed in my bag," she explained, "just like he peed on my family's antique Fateh rug. Do you by any chance sell doggy diapers?"

"No. I don't believe in them."

"Don't believe in them? Then how do I keep him from peeing everywhere?"

"He just needs to be outdoors and have some time to figure it out," Kaz told her.

"He's already four months old. Shouldn't he have already learned?" Haley complained. "Anyway," she continued, "I have this list of things I need for taking care of Bingo."

While continuing to hold the puppy, Kaz perused the list. "Chew toys. Easy. But dog-proofing supplies? You can use child-proofing products, but you really wouldn't need those things if you just take the time to train your puppy properly."

"But that's the problem. I don't have a clue how to train a dog, and I don't have time to do it anyway," Haley said. Tears welled in her eyes.

Before Kaz's brain considered what he was about to do, his mouth made the commitment. "I'll train him for you."

"You will? How much do you charge?"

"Only that you be consistent with what I teach your puppy and that you spend ten minutes each day with him and me, starting tonight. Bring him at closing time." He handed the puppy back to her. "Deal?"

"Deal."

At home in the great room, Haley set up a plastic exercise pen that she bought from the pet shop, lifted Bingo into the enclosure, and handed the puppy a dried pig ear to chew, though she told herself that it was plastic because she couldn't stand the idea of touching a pig's ear. "Good doggy!" she said, hoping that it would be true, and then she poured a glass of chilled pinot grigio and waited for the truck from the carpet cleaning company to arrive.

A phone call from Brent and the doorbell ring arrived simultaneously, which made it very difficult to direct the rug removal while masking the reason for its removal from Brent. While writing on a piece of paper, "dog pee," and handing the paper to the rug guy, she said to Brent on the phone, "Yes, I dropped a soda, and it splattered onto my Aunt Alice's rug … I know! It's a disaster!"

Then she signed the paperwork for the rug cleaning, as the guy mouthed the word, "Soda?" and grinned.

Haley gave him a warning look and continued the conversation with Brent, "No, it's okay. You don't need to come over … No, really. Bingo and I are just relaxing on the back deck."

The rug guy gave her a thumbs-up, and carried the rolled rug to his van.

She closed the front door. "Well, if you insist. Sure, I'll have some mojitos for us." Haley quickly clicked off the phone. "Oh shit!" she bellowed to the empty house. She grabbed Bingo, who still clung to his wet, soggy, chewed pig's ear, and, dropping her cell phone onto the kitchen counter, took the dog and its toy out to the back deck. "Stay!" she commanded and went back into the house to mix a pitcher of mojitos. When she returned to the deck with the pitcher and two glasses, the puppy was gone.

"Bingo!" she called, rushing down the stairs. "Bingo!"

Someone down the block yelled back, "We've got a winner!"

"Ha, ha! Very funny!" she called out, glaring in the direction of the voice.

Haley looked around the yard. No dog. She looked under the hydrangea bushes. No dog. She looked under the deck. No dog.

Why did this have to happen now, when Brent was on his way to her house? She had to stop him. Frantically she tried to invent a story as she rushed up the steps to retrieve her iPhone from the kitchen. But before she reached the door, she heard the sound of a car pulling onto the gravel of her parking pad. Damn! Her face felt flushed and her heart was beating crazy fast. Haley sank into a deck chair, prepared to tell Brent the horrible truth. Just then, a little puff of gray and white fur appeared from behind the oversized ceramic planter in the far corner of the deck. "There you are!" She rushed over to the puppy and lifted him into the air. "What a good little puppy you are!"

"I wish I had a camera right now," Brent called up to her from the yard. "So how's motherhood going?"

At the moment, she could honestly say, "Wonderfully," as she pet Bingo on the top of his head until the puppy started squirming to be released. She was about to put him down on the deck when she saw the monstrous black dog that Brent had been walking earlier that day. Only now, that creature was in her yard. She gasped.

"No worries," Brent assured her. "He's gentle. I brought him along so he and Bingo can play while you and I hang out."

"But won't that big creature ..."

"Bear?"

"He's a bear?" Haley held the puppy closer, causing it to struggle all the more.

"No. His temporary name is Bear. He's a Mastiff. A very sweet Mastiff."

"But he's so big. Won't he hurt Bingo?"

"Bear didn't hurt him when they were roommates before I brought Bingo to you."

Haley let go of the puppy and the little thing ran down the deck stair and started running circles around Bear. Okay, she could relax. No mommy duties since Brent had supplied a canine babysitter.

Brent asked too many questions about how she and Bingo were getting along, and Haley gave short answers that kept the conversation from going in any one direction long enough for her to get caught in a lie.

A few mojitos later, Brent leaned in and kissed her. Not a "good job, dear friend" type of kiss, this kiss was so intense that even her toes were tingling. He hadn't kissed her like that since they first dated three years ago, and he certainly didn't kiss her like that during the months when their almost-engaged relationship was going down the proverbial toilet until they finally called it quits last September.

"You are full of surprises," he said.

"So are you."

"I couldn't help myself. The way you held little Bingo brought out something in you. A glow. Very sexy."

The sun had gone down before Haley remembered her deal with Kaz, a deal that she was not going to share with Brent. It would wreck the whole pretense that she was the ultimate doggy mom. And if just hugging Bingo got her a tingling make-out session, what more could she get by having Bingo show signs of training? The stakes were higher now, higher than a free weekend of shopping on Fifth Avenue. Since her breakup with Brent, she hadn't connected with any other guy on quite the same level. Now she had a chance to start over.

She pointed at Bingo and Bear, who were both napping on the deck nearby. "Brent, sweetie, I think you should go. It's been a full day for Bingo, and I'm kinda tired myself."

"Not tired of me?" he asked.

She snuggled in his arms.

"I like that answer," he said. "Maybe we can go to Sedona for dinner on Saturday and leave the dogs home."

That was a revelation. Leave the dogs home? It hadn't occurred to her that it would be okay to leave Bingo home once in a while, or at least it would be okay whenever she's doing something with Brent. "Dinner at Sedona with you? Sounds good to me."

Already, she was wondering where this was going, and whether it was a path she wanted to travel again. Of course, if they got back together, the trip to New York could be even more spectacular.

Kaz had waited an extra fifteen minutes for the girl to show up. He shook his head. She wasn't the right person to foster a dog. She had said, "This is my first and last." In Kaz's opinion, that should be settled quickly. He would contact Brent tomorrow to adopt the little Havanese.

Haley, out of breath, showed up at the shop just before Kaz clicked the dead-bolt lock into place. "I'm so sorry," she said. "I had company, and I had to get them to leave before I could come. It won't happen again. I promise."

The girl seemed sincere, so he'd hold off on talking with Brent. He noticed that Bingo was nodding off in her arms. "It looks like your puppy got some exercise today. Good. We'll keep this first lesson short."

Haley started to hand him the dog.

"No, no. He must get used to a leash." Kaz connected a leash to Bingo's collar and put him on the floor. The dog looked confused, but when Kaz started to walk to the door, Bingo followed.

"Where are we going?" Haley asked.

"The Assembly Grounds. The field is big enough to train a curious puppy."

"Couldn't we just train Bingo here in your shop?" she asked.

Kaz was concerned. Was this girl hiding something? And he was a bit uncomfortable with the idea of being alone with this young woman inside his shop after hours. "Okay, but only for this first lesson, and I'll keep the door unlocked, yes?"

Bingo's energy returned when he smelled the beefy treat Kaz

held out to the puppy. The training began, and what was supposed to be a ten-minute lesson actually ran thirty minutes, but by the end, Bingo knew two important commands: sit and stay.

"You must practice often with him. This may save his life one day," Kaz told her.

"And mine, too," she said. "I wish Bingo had known these commands earlier today."

For the next few weeks, Haley learned more than dog commands and safety tips from Kaz. She listened as the old man shared his philosophy about respect for animals and the duty to take care of what cannot care for itself. It certainly made things complicated for her. How could she keep up this training while all the while not being honest with Kaz about her motives? And there was another reason for her to step away from the daily sessions: She was finding it more and more difficult to get to the shop for the training lessons; Bear had been adopted and Brent had started spending more and more time at her house, focused on other pursuits like getting Haley into bed. Not that she was complaining about that. The romance had kindled and was in full flame now, and she was enjoying every hot moment of it.

"I have a surprise for you. We're going to New York this weekend," Brent whispered into her ear as they lay on the sofa of the great room. "I've already booked a room."

Haley was indeed surprised, but not in the way that Brent may have expected. Sure, she had been waiting for this trip to Manhattan, but it was supposed to happen at the end of the dare. "So I won the dare?" she asked.

"It doesn't matter now," he said to her. "Now that we're together, who cares about it?"

"I do."

"Okay, then you won the dare."

Haley didn't like the "whatever" tone in his voice. "You say that like you don't mean it."

He pulled her closer. "Of course I mean it. It's just that our getting back together became more important to me than a stupid game, so I stopped thinking about the dare." Then he scrunched his eyebrows together. "It's the same for you, right? You weren't playing me to win a stupid dare, were you?"

Haley jumped off the sofa. "Of course not! Getting back together with you has been great. It's the best thing that could have happened. But it's not part of the New York deal. I worked hard with Bingo to win that trip to Manhattan, and I don't want it to just be a weekend away with my boyfriend."

Brent sat up and looked at her with an "aha" in his eyes. He grinned. "I forgot how competitive you are. You're right. New York is your win. I have to admit that I never thought you'd succeed at fostering a dog, but you did it. So, are you willing to take that trip this weekend?"

"If I can find someone to take care of Bingo with such short notice, then of course."

Haley was surprised and quite nervous when Brent suggested that they go to the pet store. She wished she had told Kaz her secret, but it was too late for that now. She'd have to prepare a spin on whatever might be said at the shop.

Inside Kaz's store, Brent said to Haley, "Now that the dare is over, you can stop fostering the dog. Kaz is going to adopt him." He lifted Bingo onto the counter in front of Kaz, and Bingo started licking the old man's hand.

Haley felt like she'd been struck. She hadn't prepared a spin for this situation, and she didn't know what to say. She was shocked by the possibility that Kaz may have been in on this all along. No wonder he spent so much energy on training Bingo.

"Is this what you want, Haley?" the old man asked.

Sure, it had started out that way. When the dog had peed on the rug, she was ready to give him away to anyone, but, during the weeks that followed, her relationship to the dog had changed. Bingo followed her from room to room and sat on her lap while she watched television. He licked her ankles and cuddled close to her feet when she sat at the computer writing her fashion blog. He entertained her with his squeaky toys. But there was one thing Bingo did that meant the most. He gave her his paw every morning like a greeting. The paw. She and Kaz had never taught Bingo to do that. It just happened one morning. And then it happened every morning. It was like a gift from Bingo, a special bonding ritual they shared.

"Is this what you want, Haley?" Kaz repeated.

Bingo sat up on his hind legs and waved his paws at her.

Haley grabbed her puppy and held him close. "No," she answered. "Bingo is my dog."

The old man nodded. "Yes, he is. He is your dog."

Haley heard the sincerity in his voice. She realized now that this whole plan had totally been Brent's idea. She turned and glared at her boyfriend, "Did you really think that I would be okay about this?"

Brent was speechless. He looked from Haley to Kaz to Haley. Then he shrugged. "Okay. I was wrong. You've changed, Haley. I guess I have a lot to learn about you."

"Yes, you do."

"Maybe a weekend in New York would be a good start?" he asked.

Haley hugged the puppy. "Do the hotels allow dogs? I was hoping to carry Bingo around in a Louis Vuitton like Paris Hilton would," she said. Seeing that Kaz did not find this amusing, she added, "Only kidding."

"Haley, Bingo wouldn't be happy in New York," Kaz said. "I'll gladly dog-sit for you."

She handed the puppy to Kaz. "You know, just because Bingo's my dog, doesn't mean you have to be out of the picture, Kaz. We could think of you as Bingo's uncle."

The old man shook his head. "Now, Haley, you know how I feel about pet ownership. I'll always have time for Bingo, but he doesn't have to be treated as though some other species is better than his own canine family."

Brent laughed. "Relax, Kaz. There are worse roles you could be given. At least Bingo isn't a monkey; then you'd be a monkey's uncle."

Kaz groaned at the stupid joke, while Haley nudged Brent. "And you," she said. "Be sure to work out. I expect that you will be carrying a lot of shopping bags."

The old man handed a treat to Bingo and said to the dog. "Wy jesteście kochani."

Haley asked, "What did you say to him?"

The old man smiled. "You are loved. Wy jesteście kochani."

Haley sounded out the phrase, "Vih yes-tesh-che ko-han-nee."

Brent smiled at her, ""Vih yes-tesh-che ko-han-nee."

Haley was glad that she hadn't played the quit ticket this time; she figured that the universe can owe her one in the future. In the meantime, she planned to collect on everything Brent owed her and more.

Shifting Sands

Taking Sides

Guess what! You guys will never believe, I found out that it only costs $250 to bury a cat. So I figured, why don't I just put my step-monster into a large cat suit?

> —spoken by Demi Moore as the character Jules in *St. Elmo's Fire*

Propping your right foot against a boardwalk bench, you finish a quick stretch before your morning walk. Your mind is miles away. You're meeting your dad's new wife for the first time today, and what runs through your mind is Demi Moore and *St. Elmo's Fire.*

Dad is on the way from his condo in New York to your Ocean City beach house for his annual June visit. Typically, you would have given up your walk to prepare for him. You would have prepped some fresh fruit to make his favorite summer pancakes and would have set the table with the hand-painted blue striped breakfast plates that he and your mom brought back from England for your birthday present five summers ago, the year you bought the beach house. But today, he's bringing the new Mrs. Coldwell, the replacement for your mom, whom he divorced last December. Merry Christmas! Here's your very first step-monster, sweetie!

You reach into your wristband for another Pepcid AC. The chalky sweet pieces crumble and then melt on your tongue, leaving the promised berry flavor. Ready to get going, you look (as though entering a highway) before you take your place in the early morning flow of boardwalk walkers.

The boardwalk is busy this morning, a sign that the summer season is in full swing. It seems that everyone has been watching *The Dr. Oz Show* and has been bitten by the exercise bug. You glance face to face, checking off the regulars. You know them, not by name, but by their signature trait. "Pink Sneakers" wears her blond hair tied back into a ponytail with a Hello Kitty ribbon that matches the laces in her shoes. "Shaved Head" likes to cut the sleeves off his shirts and ties a faded red bandana around his bald head like a sweatband. "His And Hers" dress alike in navy sweats with white piping. "iPod Zombie" always stares straight ahead, listening to who-knows-what.

What do they call you? Are you "Terrapins Baseball Cap"? You'd like that name. Your undergraduate years at the University of Maryland were great times, especially the nightlife at the College Park bars that were within walking (or stumbling) distance from the campus. You've heard that your favorite one lost its liquor license a few years ago. They should have carded better. You remember the night your friends took you there to celebrate your twenty-first birthday, your official "being legal," and the look on the face of the bartender when he realized that he'd been serving you all semester. You smiled at him and sang out, "Cheers!" Now it's just a food joint. You sigh because that was where you had your first beer, your first vodka, your first tequila, your first hangover. How did you ever manage to maintain a 3.8 GPA and graduate magna cum laude? But you did. You had to. Your parents both graduated from Maryland and that made you a "legacy" with reputations to honor.

Your parents were the ultimate collegiate couple. They were even married in Memorial Chapel on campus. The bridesmaids, your mom's sorority sisters, carried the Maryland state flower, black-eyed Susan, in their bouquets, and the outdoor reception was held under a huge tent on the grounds of Fraternity Row.

That was never your dream. Neither was sorority life. You didn't pledge to your mom's sorority, despite her constant prodding (or maybe because of her prodding), but though you'd refused to become a sorority sister, your mom still kept her fingers crossed that you would at least catch a husband before graduation and follow in her footsteps. Another disappointment for Mom. And now this: Dad rebounded before she did.

Last night, your mom called from the winter house in Florida. (Dad got the New York condo for its proximity to his law office.) "How are you doing? How's the weather? Married yet?" Her typical intro to any conversation with you.

And you gave your routine answer, "Fine. Warm. No." As always, she sidestepped the real reason for the call, holding out long enough to drive you crazy and force you into a game of read-my-mind, a game in which she'd win gold if it were an Olympic sport. Eventually, you just told her, rushing through the words to keep her from interrupting and prolonging the discussion. "Yes, Dad is bringing the new wife. No, it wouldn't be a good idea for you to join us. Please wait until mid-July. You'll have me all to yourself that way. No drama. We'll shop the outlets. We'll do a day trip to Cape May. We'll do whatever you want. Just not now."

The memory of the conversation makes your blood pressure spike. Take in a deep breath of salt air and try to relax. Keep walking. Think about your new walking shoes and how great they feel. Wonder whether the other regulars have noticed that you've switched to navy blue sneakers, not that it matters except that you'd notice if they made any changes.

Changes. Like anyone, you really aren't thrilled with changes unless they're your own doing. You wonder if Dad's new wife will want to join you and your dad for the morning walk ritual. Resentment burns up your throat. Pop another antacid. Maybe you should pretend that you don't do a morning walk anymore. Let them walk on their own, if that's what they want. You want no part of it. You imagine how they would look in this parade of boardwalk walkers. Your dad would wear his usual outfit, white tennis shorts and the green rugby shirt he got in London. Then you imagine Mrs. Coldwell. *Mrs. Coldwell?* There's only one Mrs. Coldwell in your mind, and that's your mother, Patrice Coldwell. You'll call your dad's new wife by her first name: Charlene. You see Charlene in Chico's cropped linen Bermuda shorts with a matching blouse, like what she was wearing in that photograph your dad emailed. They were sitting on a wall at a scenic spot in the Grand Canyon. You wish she'd fallen off and been tossed from rock to rock to her death. The obituary would read: "Mrs. Charlene Coldwell, very briefly the wife of Mr. Jonathan Coldwell and beloved mother of Lulu and Lolly (her teacup poodles), fell to her death in a freak accident at the Grand Canyon."

You smile. You enjoyed killing off Charlene in your mind. The daydream continues. Your mom would come to the funeral out of respect for her ex-husband, who would rush into her arms and beg to be taken back. He'd tell her that Charlene was a bitch who had tricked him into the marriage in hopes of getting his money. You remember that in the photograph her left hand was glittering from what was probably a diamond ring. Money grubber!

You glance down at your watch: 8:05 a.m. When your dad called, he was pulling onto Route 1 from I-95. You estimate the time it should take for your dad to drive from Christiana to the beach house on 56th Street. You have enough time to make a full walk of the boardwalk as long as you keep up your pace. Count off the blocks as you speed past each street number.

Pink Sneakers has been joined by an older guy. His gray hair puts him at fifty or so, though he's trying to look like he's not.

He's wearing a new pair of gym shorts and a Sex Wax T-shirt that is too tight for his aging physique and does not convince anyone that he can actually ride a surfboard. He seems to be trying to impress Pink Sneakers.

Suddenly, the guy looks too much like your father. You stop walking, pull out your iPhone, and open the Find My Friends app. It shows that your father is getting close to Kent County. You wipe the sweat from your face with the edge of your T-shirt. Maybe you should get home and finish prepping for their arrival.

A quick checkup of the townhouse helps you prioritize what still needs to be done to prepare for your company. Towels for the guest bath. Wildflowers for the bedroom. Snacks for their arrival. You write it all down. In your current state of mind, you're sure to forget something. And you almost did—Take a shower!

You reach into the linen closet for the new Ralph Lauren red, white, and blue Egyptian cotton towels for the guest bathroom, but your attention is grabbed by another set of towels—white ones with your parents' initials monogrammed in navy blue silk threads. You had these made before you found out that your parents were splitting up. You had considered giving them to a local thrift store, but now you almost do a cheerleading jump (not that you'd ever done a cheerleading jump) at the good fortune that had them still folded in this closet. Putting on a face of innocence (even though there's no one to observe your acting skills), you place the towels on the towel rack with the monograms prettily displayed. "Oops!" you sing.

Check the phone app again. They're halfway through Kent County now. Your dad has such a lead foot. Should you give him a quick call to remind him of the speed traps on Route 1? When you consider that his being pulled over for a ticket could buy you more time before having to meet Charlene, you decide not to call him. Serves him right for replacing Mom.

You arrange flowers in a vase that belonged to your mother's mother, and place it on the bureau of the guest bedroom. Smile at yourself in the mirror. This is fun.

Dump some crackers and chips into matching bowls, and make some crab dip, hoping Charlene might have a shellfish allergy. Chill a bottle of sauvignon blanc, and decide to finish off the open bottle of riesling while you wait for the inevitable arrival of the step-monster. Be glad that you're on your own and don't have to call her "Mom."

Two glasses of riesling later, you drink the last drops from the bottle and drop it into the recycle can. Check the phone app again and feel the jolt of dread—your dad's car is turning at the 56th Street traffic light at the end of your block and you didn't take your shower yet. Rush outside to the deck, tripping over the sliding glass door frame. Try to not fall face-first onto the jute rug and receive a semi-permanent skin burn. Reach for the café table, knocking over a pot of daisies and sending potting soil everywhere. Get your balance in time to watch him drive up to your garage door in a shiny red convertible Lexus. Roll your eyes. Midlife crisis?

Your dad waves to you. His passenger, who is wearing a scarf around her hair and sunglasses like she thinks she's Audrey Hepburn, smiles and waves, too, but you just click open the garage door and sweep the scattered potting soil off the table, the rug, and the deck, hoping that your dad's car got into the garage before the stream of dirt landed on the ground below.

Take a deep breath, and go inside to wait for Dad and the movie star to climb the stairs from the garage below. Your first words to them are, "So where are Lulu and Lolly?"

"They're at summer camp," Charlene says, and extends her hand to you. "You must be Wendy."

"I guess I must," you say.

Your dad gives you the knock-it-off eyebrows and puts his arm around his new wife. "And this lovely woman is Charlene."

You smile like a good girl, and gesture to the tray of munchies. "I hope you like crab dip."

"I love crab dip," says Charlene. "I grew up just outside DC and love anything made with crab. Jon promised that we can have some steamed crabs while we're here. It's what I miss the most since I moved north. No one else steams the Maryland way with rock salt and Old Bay. Manhattan has great restaurants, but no one there knows how to cook a crab properly."

Damn! No chance of anaphylaxis.

You carry the snacks and chilled wine to the deck while your dad and the replacement wife deposit their bags in the guest room.

"Your home is beautiful," Charlene says. "And being so close to the boardwalk and beach is such a plus."

"Yeah, I have a great view of puking teenagers during senior week."

Once again, your dad comes to the rescue of his new bride. "So the two weeks of graduation mayhem is what you most equate to the value of owning prime real estate? Then why didn't you just buy a place on the other side of Assawoman Bay in a nice, quiet residential neighborhood like Ocean Pines?"

You get it. No messing with the step-monster. You pour the wine and make nice. "May you enjoy your stay in Ocean City!" A safe toast. No sarcasm. You wanted to say, "May you get the vacation you deserve," but you know your dad would catch the meaning. The glasses clink, and everyone seems satisfied.

The conversation over the crab dip and wine is basically pleasant, though awkwardness hangs over the chitchat. You learn that Charlene is a successful businesswoman, that she is a widow, and that your dad used to play golf with her now-deceased husband. You wonder if there had been an affair while your dad was still married and Charlene's spouse was still alive. You imagine your dad sneaking off for some afternoon delight with Charlene, and later Charlene's husband being found dead of unknown causes, but you know that your dad is not a murderer and most likely not a cheater either. So, if their relationship had been a casual friendship, how and when did Charlene and your dad hook up? Was it at the funeral parlor right there in front of the dead body? Did they lean against the casket for their first kiss? Yuck. You have a silent laugh inside, but you shut down the daydream when you realize that Dad is asking you where you'd like to have dinner tonight.

You shrug. "Wherever."

"How about Ruth's Chris Steakhouse?" he asks. Wow! He is either aiming to impress his new wife, or he's trying to buy your cooperation for the next two weeks. Dinner at Ruth's Chris would definitely score either way.

After suggesting some beach time, you wipe down with a washcloth, get into your skimpiest bikini to test both your dad and Charlene, and lead the way to a spot near the ocean. While the happy couple sits under a rental umbrella, you place your quilt in direct sunlight and lather on minimum sunscreen. Considering your dad's grimace at the lack of fabric in your swimsuit, you think you may have gone too far and realize what a challenge the next two weeks are going to be. Make an effort to appease him by creating some small talk. "So the dogs have summer camp?"

Charlene explains that it's just a way of saying that they're being taken care of by their groomer. It seems like she wants to tell you more about Lulu and Lolly, but she stops at the end of her sentence.

"So will you buy Lucy and Lacy doggy shirts with 'My parents went to Ocean City and all I got was this stupid T-shirt' printed on them?"

Dad jumps in with, "No, *Lulu* and *Lolly* will not get doggy shirts, and if I had my way, they'd be here at the ocean with us.

I wanted to ask you, but Charlene wouldn't let me, even though being without them for two weeks is quite a sacrifice for us."

"I wouldn't be so rude as to take my pets to someone's house," she explains.

Okay, so she's considerate. Your mom would have brought the dogs just to make a point. Score one for the step-monster. And Charlene has her own career, so she might not be with Dad for his money. Another score. But she's the reason that your parents are no longer together, right? Penalty two points. She's back to zero.

Your cell phone dings, signaling a message. You see that your mom has texted: "Is the home wrecker there yet?"

You click off the phone.

It doesn't take long for you to realize that your dad told Charlene a lot about you. She asks about your promotion to associate professor and your dissertation on wetland conservation. You're impressed with the level of her questions and her apparent understanding. She says that her love of the ocean has always made her interested in saving the coastline. She gets her points back. Your dad's face beams. As much as you don't want to like this woman, you can sort of see her appeal. Decide to dial down the smart-ass attitude.

When your dad goes into the water for a swim, an opportunity arises. "So how long have you and my dad been together?" You had to ask it.

"As a couple? Not until after your parents' divorce was finalized." She watches your father as he swims parallel to the shoreline, then she quickly acknowledges the elephant in the room. "Wendy, I didn't break up your parents' marriage. When my husband was in hospice care, he asked your dad to look after me when he was gone and to make sure that I was doing okay. Your dad kept his promise. He helped me handle the insurance companies' paperwork, and he made sure that I had good legal and financial support through the same advisors he and your mom were using. That's all. After your mom left him, Jon and I occasionally had dinner together."

Mom left Dad? That's news to you. You'd always thought it was the other way around.

"We were just friends who didn't want to eat alone," Charlene adds. "I didn't even think he was interested in me until he brought it up one afternoon when we went to see a show."

You believe her, even though you don't want to. Deep inside, you wanted to be able to blame her for the destruction of your neat little family, but she doesn't seem to be the witch you thought she was. Or hoped she was. Your mom certainly painted that picture for you in vivid witchy detail, but now you have to wonder. You think about times in your own life when a relationship crashed and you referred to your ex-boyfriend as scum of the earth, especially if that scum found a new girlfriend before you had a new boyfriend. Blame it on human nature.

The cell phone dings again with another message from Mom: "No answer? Did the witch eat you?"

You pretend it's a work colleague, and type into the phone: "Stop it. Call you later."

As you start to put the phone into your beach bag, it dings again. Curiosity makes you check it. "She's right there, isn't she?"

You turn off the phone. "They can't seem to understand that I'm on vacation," you say to Charlene, hoping she believes your lie.

Charlene isn't paying attention to you at all. She's staring out at the ocean, watching your father show off his swimming skills. Oh my God! Charlene thinks your dad's sexy. The stepmonster—the witch—totally fades away, and in her place you see a woman in love, gazing at her lover. And that lover happens to be your father. Wow. That's an image you need to erase from your mind before you need psychotherapy.

Shifting Sands

Break the thought. Grab the beach bag and pull out the Sudoku book you bought at Mason's. You turn the pages to the next unsolved puzzle, but your attention darts to the shoreline and your Dad exiting the water. You watch him emerge from the ocean like Charlton Heston in *From Here to Eternity*, with rivulets of water running down his muscled chest, while Charlene, leaning forward in the beach chair, seems to be having a hot flash; her face is in full blush.

Oh, my God! You feel like a voyeur. You expect them to fall to the sand together and have wild passionate sex right there in front of the whole world. Worse, in front of you! Focus on your puzzle. Scribble "3" in an obvious space, and check for other places to put that number. Damn! You can't even do a math puzzle when your mind is fighting you. Toss the book back into the beach bag and say, "So, Dad, isn't it time that we get ready for dinner?"

He towels off, and leans into Charlene for a kiss. Take a mental photo of the moment and imagine it on the cover of a Harlequin romance. Become aware of your own ridiculously small bikini and feel the urgent need to cover up, but you didn't bring anything but a spare towel. Wrap it around your suit like a terrycloth sarong, grab your phone, and ask Siri to search for the phone number of the restaurant, all the while trying not to watch your dad and Charlene. "I'd better call ahead for a reservation. They book up quickly during the summer." As though anyone wouldn't already know this. But before you can reach the restaurant, you see a final text message from your mom: "You can't ignore me, dearie."

Uh-oh. When mom calls someone "dearie," it usually means trouble.

The walk back to the house is interesting. Dad and Charlene hold hands, and you hope that the next two weeks are going to feel less awkward, that maybe you'll eventually adjust to the affectionate gestures between these two. That dream is dashed when you hear a loud female voice sing out, "Helloooooo!"

"What the hell is she doing here?" your dad says.

You look up to the second-floor deck and see your mom waving a martini glass. "How is everybody?"

Remember that both your parents have keys to your home. Say to your dad, "Please believe me. She wasn't invited."

"She invited herself," your dad says loud enough that everyone on the block could hear him. "Inconsiderate and self-absorbed, as always."

"That's not nice, Jon," your mom calls out. "I just wanted to meet your new wife and spend some time with our daughter. You and I have always spent these two weeks in June with her. Why should that change just because you got yourself another woman?"

Your face burns with embarrassment. Now that you're starting to like Charlene, you're upset that your mom would act this way. She's making herself look foolish, but you wait until you're inside the condo to continue any conversation with her.

Mom gives a sloppy self-introduction to Charlene, following it with, "Oh, but you know who I am. We met at Robert's funeral, right?"

Charlene politely agrees and even thanks Mom for the beautiful flower arrangement that she sent.

"Really? You liked the peonies?" my mother asks.

"You mean tulips," Charlene says, not falling into the trap. "You sent tulips. In a crystal vase. They were beautiful. I still have the vase."

Mom is not a graceful loser, so Dad quickly interrupts with the suggestion that everyone shower and get ready so he can take all of us out to Ruth's Chris Steakhouse. He emphasizes "all of us" which causes Mom to raise her eyebrows and say, "Isn't that classy of you, Jon!"

"Why, yes, I do believe it is," your dad says; then he exits into the guest suite with Charlene.

Finally alone, you confront your mother. "Weren't you in Key Largo last night? And didn't I say that I didn't want you to come while they're here?"

"You may have, but I didn't agree. And I think it's very disrespectful of you to take sides like this."

"Well, Mom, I wasn't taking sides … until now." You start toward the master bedroom, but stop to ask, "By the way, how did you manage to get here from Florida so quickly?"

"A friend with a plane. He flew me to the Ocean City Airport this morning, and I got a cab from there. What's the big deal? You have plenty of room, and I don't mind sleeping out here in the great room. This is a sleep sofa, right?" Mom lifts up one of the cushions. "Just give me some sheets, and I'll cover the mattress; that is, unless you were planning to offer me your master bedroom suite."

Of course she'd play that card. But she underestimated how pissed you are. "No, Mom, that wasn't my plan."

"So I'll be roughing it like that dreadful time your dad and I took you camping in the Appalachians so you could earn that Girl Scout badge. Mosquitoes bit every inch of my body, but you got your badge. My back was so wrecked from sleeping on an air mattress that I had to visit the chiropractor for a month afterwards. But anything for my little girl."

"This isn't an air mattress. It's a Jennifer Convertibles sofa with a top-quality mattress," you snap at her. "You won't get any back pain from sleeping on this sofa, though I might experience a pain in my neck, or maybe a pain in my butt, during your stay."

"Aren't you the witty one," Mom remarks.

"I get it from you. You taught me well."

"You're welcome. And I assume that I share the guest bathroom with Jon and whatever-her-name-is?"

"Charlene. You know that her name is Charlene. And since you'll be seeing her a lot in the future, you need to stop playing that game." Feel a touch of guilt knowing that you played that same game earlier by purposely messing up the dog names. Like mother, like daughter.

"Why are you being so mean to me, Wendy?"

"Because, Mom, you've made a mess of things. This was supposed to be my time with Dad. It was going to be difficult enough for me because I had to let go of my dream that you and he would get back together. I had planned to be a brat to Charlene and send a clear message that I didn't intend to be a friendly stepchild. But it seems that she's not the step-monster I expected. She's actually very nice. If you had just stayed in Florida, I might have been able to get the whole picture and make a decision of where she fits in or doesn't fit into my life. But you dropped in uninvited and created a situation that forces me to compare the two of you. Frankly, Mom, you're not making a very good case for yourself."

"Oh," is all your mother says.

Though your mom has always been a wall, you think of how embarrassing this whole situation might be for her. The guilt begins to gnaw at you, so you make the offer that you hadn't planned. "You can have my room; I'll sleep out here."

Your mom shakes her head. "No. I rather like the idea of the sofa bed. Closer to the liquor cabinet, my dear. "

"My dear" seems lighter than "dearie," but you won't take any chances, so you say, "I'll get some linens and make up the sofa for you."

"No. You go take your shower. I know where you keep the linens. Besides, I'm going to need another drink if I'm expected to behave at dinner."

More liquor doesn't guarantee your mom's behavior. Sometimes she's the gregarious hostess, while other times, she's a surly bitch. "My dear" or "dearie"? Prepare yourself to be either the diplomat or the referee.

You pick up her suitcase and bags. "I'll put these in my room, since you'll be sharing my bathroom during your visit."

"Oh, damn, I was hoping to share the guest bathroom with Jon and Charlene, and find that we get along so wonderfully that we'd have a threesome and live happily ever after."

"Happily? Fat chance, Mom."

"Who are you calling 'fat'?" she asks with mock hurt.

You sigh in relief. This is the fun mom, the one you enjoy being around, so you say, "Not you." Your mom has always maintained her size-eight body and has kept her plastic surgeon well paid for keeping her face youthful enough to match that body. That's one thing you admire about your mom—she takes care of herself. Well dressed. Manicured. She can walk in three-inch heels without a wobble. And still a honey blonde.

In comparison, Charlene is average. Size twelve and some silver peeking from her dark hair. Yet attractive. And infinitely sweeter than your mom. Go figure.

Before you escape into the shower, you hear your mom singing "This One's for the Girls." You didn't think your mom even listened to country music, yet she's singing a McBride hit at the top of her voice, obviously attempting to serenade her ex-husband and the new wife, like laying down a challenge. A chill runs up your spine, and you plead to the heavens that what seems to be an inevitable catfight won't happen at dinner.

Thank God your dad picked the right place for this first family meal. Ruth's Chris is so elegant that the atmosphere has set the right tone for courteous behavior. The only competition you can see is one of fashion and style. Mom is decked out in a sleek body-hugging black cocktail dress with gold dangling hoop earrings and a gold cuff bracelet; Charlene wears an A-line purple dress, sexy in a conservative, yet flattering, way, with a floral silk scarf that brings attention to her breasts, which are much larger than your mom's. (Way to go, Charlene!) So the runway battle is between thin, small-boobed, bottle-blonde Mom vs. gracefully aging Raquel Welch.

Dad plays along, saying to the waiter, "What a lucky man I am. Dinner with three beautiful women. What more could a guy want?"

What more could he want? How about an ex who moves on with her life? That would be great. Or at least a calm dinner without any drama-induced heartburn? A steak without a mistake. You and your dad sit opposite one another at the table, like fans at a tennis match. You are both waiting for the start of the game, numbing your nerves with some gin and tonic.

Since their assets cancel each other out, physical attributes can't be the source of this Past Wife vs. Present Wife challenge. Instead, the focus of the game becomes witty repartee. Mom leads with comments about website commerce (trying to hit Charlene in her business zone), while stepmom counters with digs about women who enjoy being kept by their men rather than cultivating careers of their own (in reference, of course, to how your mom never got around to using her license to practice law). Then, Mom offers fake sympathy for women who never gave birth (knowing that Charlene has no children), and stepmom delivers a punch with how sad it is that some women never had the opportunity to develop themselves and their God-given talents (using the "God-given" descriptor to give more weight to your mom's inability to be financially self-sufficient, a statement that implies that Charlene knows every detail of Mom's dependence on Dad's alimony). Surprisingly, the implied insults in these rounds seem less important than the quality of fancy phrasing. You can actually see some glimmer in the eyes of each woman as her counterpart tosses off each thinly-veiled slight with vocabulary that would impress Dorothy Parker, the writer who once said about herself, "The first thing I do in the morning is brush my teeth and sharpen my tongue."

Of course, the amount of alcohol being consumed and the superb food lighten the tone of the evening. By the time the crème brûlée is served, your mom and your stepmom are chatting away like college roommates.

You and your dad toast, while your mom and stepmom accompany each other to the ladies room. When they return, Charlene shocks you with, "So, Wendy, when are you going to find yourself a husband?"

Mom almost knocks over her water glass. "That's exactly what I've been asking her for years."

Charlene winks at you, and you know that this is part of her strategy to build a friendly, though somewhat phony, relationship with the ex-wife.

This would be okay with you, but then your dad (who doesn't seem to have a clue that his new wife is not being sincere) joins in. "Wendy, I know how hard it is to be alone, and how difficult it is to meet ..." (You know that he stopped himself from saying "the right person.") He continues with, "... someone. I worry about you going through life without a partner. Have you tried any of the online dating services?"

You feel put on the spot, as though all three of them are ganging up on you now, or at least the biological ones are. Okay, you can play the game, too. "I guess it's time that I told you all ... (heavy pause to mimic your dad's comment) ... something." You take a long sip of your drink as though preparing to deliver a difficult piece of information. "I'm thinking of joining a convent."

Your dad, who has been through enough today to cause any other man to drop over, looks confused, like he's halfway between laughing and crying. "Seriously, Wendy?" he asks with eyes widened.

You laugh so hard that gin and tonic rushes from your nose, and you have to cover your face with a napkin.

"Oh come on, Jon! You believed her? Can you imagine Wendy taking a vow of poverty?" your mom says.

"Or a vow of silence?" Charlene adds.

Your dad looks at his wife and his ex-wife, and then he gets a big smile on his face. He calls the waiter over, and suggests ending dinner with a special wine. You wonder what your dad is up to, but you're sure it's more than a desire for wine.

The waiter hands him the wine list, and your dad pulls out his reading glasses and peruses the list. Then, he gives a dramatic sigh. "It's not on the list," he complains.

The waiter is visibly upset. "Are you sure, sir? We have an extensive wine cellar. Perhaps we can find a similar vintage? Which wine were you hoping to find?"

"Do you have any Blue Nun?"

That's it! Everyone at the table explodes with laughter, and the poor waiter turns ashen. Dad, seeing the effect of his joke on the young man, explains, "It's just a joke. Bring a bottle of Dom Pérignon. I must toast the women in my life."

Defying Demon's Hollow

T he industrial fence, the No Trespassing sign, the haphaz-
ard piles of demolition refuse, laughed at Karen. Jenkin's
Pier had been closed down, and most of its amusements
had been dismantled and set aside, much like Karen's plans.

Four years ago, she had returned to Wildwood, New Jersey,
to face two monsters: her fortieth birthday and a ride called
Demon's Hollow. She had believed that both would slip by easily, once she slid behind the bar of one of the metal cars of the
ride-through spook house, once she faced down the ghosts of
her childhood memories and the shame of being the butt of her
cousin Sarah's teasing. *Scaredy cat! Scaredy cat! Karen is a scaredy
cat!* But Demon's Hollow hadn't given her a second chance; it
had become just a boarded-up building beyond a fenced barrier.
She had slid her fingers through the metal links of the ten-foot
fence and felt disappointment—and maybe relief—that one of
her monsters lived no more.

Though the ride had remained standing, she had seen that
Demon's Hollow was crumbling away. The portico of the ride
had been battered by the nor'easter storms that rushed from
the Atlantic Ocean every fall, and the devil, whose arms spread
over the archway, had lost a finger or two and part of its green
horns. A metal car clung to the rusty tracks, its faded leather
upholstery speckled by the sun's daily torture. Even after the
other rides had been dismantled and sold in pieces to amusement
parks, Demon's Hollow had remained, because Demon's Hollow
couldn't be recycled; it was a building, and like the other build-

ings—the arcade stands, the carnival candy shop, the motorcycle stunt stage—it had been left to rot and await demolition.

She had asked a barker, whose Dunk-the-Fool booth stood just beyond the pier on the boardwalk proper, why the pier was closed. Between the jeers of the fool, the barker had said simply, "Owner died," and then continued his call of "Dunk the fool! Put his ass in the tank. Come on. Dunk the fool!"

Karen returned each summer and stared at the abandoned ride through the fence links as though she still might defeat the monster, even though the only battle she could wage was in her mind. Secretly, she kept hoping that on her next pilgrimage to Wildwood the ride would be gone, its demolished pieces carted off like garbage.

This year, there was no barker and no fool. The booth was gone, leaving an empty space of clean wood where the dunking booth had been. But the fence remained, and the debris beyond it remained, no sign of moving on, just more fading and more crumbling.

Karen slid her fingers through the gate of the fence, as she always did, like a kid wanting entrance to the forbidden yard, but this time, something was different. The gate was unlocked.

She looked around. It was still early in the morning, so very few people were on the boardwalk. There were only a few vacationers riding rental bicycles, and none were looking her way. She slipped through, closed the gate behind her, and scurried to a spot just past Demon's Hollow—a spot where she wouldn't be seen by any passersby.

Karen felt giddy with adventure, like the mischievous child she'd never been. She felt a surge of daring and approached the sidewall of the ride where little demons decorated the corners.

Karen touched the forehead of one. Her courage retreated and she pulled her hand back quickly, like a scared little girl expecting to be sucked into Hell.

Nothing happened.

Of course. The reasoning of a forty-four-year-old adult surfaced. She took a deep breath and touched another character, a blue imp, and marveled that these decorative figures were as bright and smooth as they had been when she was a child; they had not been destroyed by storms or sun. "I guess they've been protected by the other buildings," she speculated aloud.

"Pretty little things, aren't they?" asked a voice behind her.

Karen spun around with a gasp. She expected to face the Devil himself. Instead, she saw an elderly woman sitting on a bench behind the shell of the candy shop and looking up at her from under a wide-brimmed straw hat. She was an odd sight on this deserted pier. Dressed in a floral summer frock, wearing patent leather high heels, her polished red fingernails a contrast to the white straw bag that rested on her lap, she appeared to be waiting for someone. But how could that be? She was sitting on an abandoned pier in a place where no one would see her.

Karen exhaled. "You scared me."

The lady apologized and introduced herself as Marie. She reached into her bag and drew out a silk fan that she opened and fluttered below her face. "I love to sit out here. I can see the ocean, but nobody can see me."

Karen approached the bench and sat, easing her breath back into a normal rhythm. "So you've been able to get onto this pier before?"

"Yes. It's my favorite place. Yours, too?"

"Not favorite. More an attraction of mine. I never got the chance to ride Demon's Hollow and now it's too late," Karen explained.

"Oh, nothing is ever too late, my dear."

Surely the woman was joking. "The pier is closed, and the ride doesn't work anymore. It's been that way for years," Karen said.

The elderly woman smiled at her the way that a grandmother does when she knows a secret. "Go. Sit in the car. There's always the magic of memory."

Karen looked over at the lone car waiting on what was left of the track.

"Go on," the woman insisted. "Face your demons. That's why you're here. Only you can do it."

It was a crazy idea, but maybe it was Karen's only chance to let go of regret. She inched through the entranceway of Demon's Hollow and climbed carefully over the low railing. The broken headlights of the metal car were menacing eyes daring her, but she wouldn't back down now. One leg into the car, then the other, and she sat down, resting against the tall backrest. Nothing happened. She relaxed into the seat. She laughed at how silly her childhood fears had been. The woman was right. This was a good idea. This would certainly help her let go of that childhood shame.

Suddenly, the car lurched forward. Karen gasped. What was happening? But it was too late and too dangerous to jump from the car as it climbed up the first hill. The doors to Demon's Hollow flew open, and the car plunged into the darkness, sending Karen's mind into a frantic whirlpool of uncertainty. Demon's Hollow couldn't possibly operate anymore; it had been shut down for too many years and the only electricity still on this pier traveled from a tiny fuse box to a handful of security lights. There was no rational principle that explained how this car was moving along the track. The only explanation could be something she didn't want to believe, the same belief that had kept her from Demon's Hollow when she was a child—that the ride was possessed and she was in great peril.

Lights flashed on—flashed in her face—red, purple, orange.

She heard moaning beyond the brightness, but she couldn't see past the blinking lights. And there were voices, a mix of children's voices and those of adults. "Where are you?" "Stay in the car." "I'm scared!"

But no one was there. Just Karen.

The air became thicker as the car stirred up dust from the tracks. The voices became more urgent, more terrified. "I can't breathe." "Help me!" "Mommy!"

Karen panicked. She realized that it wasn't dust curling before the orange lights and surrounding her. It was smoke. The ride was on fire.

This time it was her voice crying out, "Help me! Somebody, help me!"

Daylight blinded her temporarily as a door flew open and the car emerged onto the roof part of the ride. Karen gulped the fresh air. "Dunk the fool! Put his ass in the tank. Come on. Dunk the fool!" The carnival sounds she heard were impossible; they came from a booth that no longer existed on the Wildwood boardwalk. I'm not really on this ride, she thought. Surely this was just a horrible nightmare and she was still asleep in the motel room. She pinched her arm, trying to wake up, but it didn't help. The car plunged down a quick hill, moved through another door, and once again rolled into the smoky darkness. "Oh my God. Oh my God," Karen whimpered.

More lights. Half-faced monsters, their crackled paint still hanging to thin plywood, swung by the car, just missing her, accompanied by a garbled soundtrack of laughter.

"Stop it! Stop it!" she screamed.

Then voices returned. These were different voices than the previous time. "Jimmy!" "Hey, Jimmy, where are you, man?" "Jimmy!" Lights came on again. Karen pushed back against the seat in fear. In the light, she saw a young man, a teenager, screaming now, sitting by the track and holding his left wrist tightly as blood squirted from the stump where his hand had been. "Jimmy!" the voices called again before the boy collapsed. The sight made Karen dizzy.

"Why are you doing this to me?" she cried out. She no longer believed it was a nightmare. It was more horrible than that. Somehow this ride was alive, and she was in it. This was no unlucky twist of fate. She was convinced that she had been lured into this ride, and that the old woman on the bench had been part of the plan. But why?

A rope dropped from the ceiling next to her and swung back and forth and back and forth, then stopped as suddenly as if someone had grabbed its end. But no one was there.

Karen was sweating and trembling as the car lurched through another set of doors and again into the flood of daylight. It slammed to a stop, throwing her forward. She jumped out and ran to the bench, enraged at the old lady's part in this terrible trick, ready to tell her off.

But Marie was gone.

Karen crumpled onto the bench and sobbed. She covered her face with her hands as though that would shake off the memories of the horror she'd seen and heard on the ride. Why had the woman done this to her?

"Are you okay, miss?"

Karen half-expected to see another mangled body, but when she looked up, she saw a young security guard standing before her.

"You do know, miss, that you're not supposed to be on this pier. Didn't you read the sign?"

She nodded, but was focused on the ride behind him.

"Are you okay?" he asked her again.

"Demon's Hollow …" she started to say, but decided that it would be useless to continue. Why would he believe her? She'd sound crazy.

"Yeah. I've heard all the stories about the ride. Never rode on it though. My parents wouldn't let me."

"Why? Is it really haunted?" she asked, trying to sound calm and conversational.

"Haunted?" He laughed. "I guess it could be, but I've never gotten that feeling when I've done my rounds." He flashed a pen light into her eyes. "Are you sure you're all right?"

She blinked her eyes and pushed his light away. "I'm okay," she lied. "Just curious about Demon's Hollow. Something bad happened there, didn't it?" She wanted answers. She needed some explanation for what she'd just experienced.

"There are a lot of legends about Demon's Hollow," he said. "But there's truth to a few of them. One season, there was an electrical fire and some kids died. The fire wasn't all that big, and it was put out fairly quickly, but they couldn't find the kids through all the smoke, and a couple of them died from inhaling toxic fumes from the burning paint." He shook his head. "Of course, the ride was reopened later that month after the repairs were completed. Just can't keep a popular ride shut down during the season. They say that the deaths just added more interest."

Karen remembered the cries of the children. Then she thought of Jimmy, "Is it true that a boy lost his hand?"

"Yeah. The son of the owner. Got his hand caught in some mechanical thing. The kid died. That added more curiosity, and the crowds came to ride through Demon's Hollow hoping to see the spirits of the dead kids and the mutilated teenager. Sick, right?"

"But eventually the ride was shut down," Karen said. "Why?"

"The owner went nuts and hung himself."

Karen remembered the swinging rope inside the ride. The sudden pull on that rope, as though someone were being hanged. Her stomach turned.

"After that, his wife shut down Demon's Hollow," the guard

said. "It's a shame because Demon's Hollow was the ride that brought the crowds to Jenkin's Pier. After the ride was shut down, the pier lost money."

"Until the wife closed down the whole pier?" Karen asked.

"No," he said. "Until the wife died."

The words made her shiver. "Of natural causes?"

"As natural as age and grief," he said.

"And now the pier just sits here unused? Why hasn't anyone restored it?"

"She died without a will, and her brothers-in-law have been fighting for ownership ever since. Greedy assholes. Until the lawyers can resolve the issue of who inherits it, the pier remains in litigation and continues to deteriorate."

"It needs to be torn down," Karen whispered.

"It won't be. Once the courts decide who gets possession of the pier, it will get cleaned up and new rides will be put on it."

"I mean that Demon's Hollow needs to be torn down." Her heart was pounding with determination.

"That won't be necessary. It'll probably cave in before the legal decision is made. That's why no one's supposed to be on this side of that fence," he said, pointing to the No Trespassing sign.

"I'm sorry. The gate was open, so I just wandered in to look around."

He looked at her in disbelief. "No, ma'am. It was locked. I just came on duty and checked it less than a half hour ago."

"But it *was* open," she insisted. "And I wasn't the only one who came in. There was an old woman sitting here."

"I didn't see anyone else," he said, looking at her as though she were hallucinating.

"You're wrong," Karen said. She stood up, but she was unsteady and felt light-headed. The guard supported her arm.

"What's your name?"

"Karen Larson. Why? Are you going to arrest me?"

"You look pale. Are you staying with someone I could contact for you?"

"I'm okay. I just … I didn't eat breakfast yet, so I'm a little wobbly. I'll get some food and be fine."

As she started to leave, he stopped her. "Miss Larson, you must have dropped this." He held out a yellowed envelope.

"No. I didn't have anything with me."

"It was under the bench and your name is on it."

She looked down at the envelope and saw her name typed across its surface in letters that had the uneven strokes of an old-fashioned typewriter. She broke the seal and removed "The Last Will and Testament of Marie Jenkins." Her hands began to shake. "This must belong to the lady who was sitting on this bench. Her name was Marie."

The security officer's eyebrows lifted in disbelief. He took the paper from her. "Marie? Marie Jenkins? Well, that can't be. Marie Jenkins was the lady who owned this pier. The one I told you about. She's been dead for six years."

Karen glared at him. "Is this some kind of sick joke?"

He examined the document. "It looks real to me. And it has your name under beneficiary. The Jenkins brothers are not going to be happy about that. You'd better get yourself a lawyer before those guys find out about this."

Karen grabbed the will from him and stared at her name written in blue fountain pen ink. This frightened her more than the ride. She tried to tear the document into two, but her hands felt like someone was holding tight to them, preventing her from ripping the paper. "I don't want this," she screamed.

The young man seemed to think she was talking to him. "You can always sign it over to someone else," he said. "Heck, I'll take it! This pier will be worth millions of dollars after a cleanup and a few new rides."

Karen looked up at the façade of Demon's Hollow. It was just an old broken-down building. But then she heard eerie music coming from inside the ride.

"Hear that?" she asked him.

"Hear what?"

"Nothing," she said. It seemed that Demon's Hollow was alive only for her.

Misty images appeared. Children's faces. Jimmy. An old man.

Karen stepped toward the ride. "I'll tear you down," she said. "You'll finally be put to rest."

The images faded away.

Karen turned to the guard. "I won't let that ride live long enough to collapse. As soon as this pier is mine, I'll have Demon's Hollow ripped apart and burned in the biggest bonfire Wildwood's ever seen."

She felt the light touch of a hand on her arm, and a woman's voice whispered into her ear. "That's why you're here. Only you can do it."

She turned to face Marie, but no one was there.

Just Things

"Lucy, we don't have time to play around. Just box the darn things and label them for the flea market." Darlene tosses a black marker into the sitting room and disappears down the hallway.

Lucy hurries to the archway dividing the sitting room from the foyer and calls to her sister, "Maybe I don't want them to go to a flea market. Maybe I want to keep them. Maybe I want to keep it all."

No answer. "I'm twenty-eight years old and my sister still bosses me around like I'm a kid," she shouts so Darlene can hear her.

She hates that Darlene dismisses her so easily; and she hates that her sister is the executor of Aunt Lydia's will and is preparing the old house for sale, never considering that Lucy might want the Cape May house to remain in the family. Not that she could afford it herself, barely able to live on her earnings from Carson's Café, and she can't count on ever receiving alimony from Hank. Whatever money he gets is probably still going into his arm.

She rubs the inside of her arm. The skin is smooth and unmarked. "But for the grace of God," she thinks, and then wonders where in her mind this expression came from. "Must be you, Aunt Lydia," she whispers into the air.

Her great-aunt's collection of glass figurines is dull this morning. Lucy lifts a tiny elephant into the sunlight that streams in narrow diagonals across the sitting room. A thin layer of dust has clouded the gleam she remembers from the summer of 1991, when she and her sister stayed here—the summer when their mother left them with Aunt Lydia in Cape May, the summer their mother flew to California to try to reconcile her marriage with Steve. Lucy stopped calling him Dad when he walked out on them.

She feels a laugh bubbling up her throat as she thinks of her mother running off to the West Coast to compete with the bronzed surfer girl Steve met at a conference in LA. The irony of it all. Her mother met Steve when he was a married man, helped him cheat on his first wife, and was naïve enough to marry him. What a fool her mother had been to think a cheater could ever be faithful, and what an idiot she was to get pregnant—twice—and believe that children would keep him tied to her.

Lucy wipes the glass elephant with the edge of her T-shirt. Her great-aunt had been so particular about the glass collection and taught her to clean each item using a flannel cloth soaked in vinegar water. Today, the figurines are dirtier than they'd ever been. Aunt Lydia is surely frowning from Heaven, if such a place exists. Lucy isn't sure on the matter. If there is a Heaven, if there is a loving God, then why has her own life been such a mess?

Lucy was fifteen when she ran away. Billy, the love of her life that year, was nineteen. It had been his idea. They had been standing behind the gymnasium sharing a smoke instead of going to classes. She had been bemoaning her grounding for getting caught "borrowing" some money from the cookie jar.

"Darlene does it all the time," she complained to Billy, as tears of injustice welled in her eyes.

He tossed the butt onto the gravel drive and took her into his arms. He told her how pretty she was. Told her she was special to him. Promised to take care of her. He said they should go to Florida where it's warm, where they could live on the beach. He said they didn't need anyone else, especially not her mother.

"After all," he said, "your mom's fucked up herself. And your sister's a bitch."

It was what she had wanted to hear.

That was the night she gave herself to him in the back seat of the blue Mustang. She didn't give a thought to what her mother had said about "it" being the special gift she should save for a husband. What a laugh! Did her mother save herself until after Steve married her?

Lucy and Billy had gotten as far as Virginia before they were caught. When she was brought home—briefly, before being sent off to the Sisters of St. Francis—her mother had grilled her.

"Are you still a good girl?" What her mother meant was, "Are you still a virgin?" Lucy let her think she was. There was no sense in getting Billy into any more trouble; he had already broken the law by taking a minor over state lines.

She never saw Billy after that day, nor had she heard from him. She never knew whether the nuns had kept him away or he had just gone off on his own, relieved that he hadn't ended up in a jail cell doing time for their little adventure. She often wondered what had become of him.

"What are you doing?" Darlene asks from the archway of the foyer.

Lucy holds out the figurine. "Remember how long it took to clean these?"

"No. I never had to clean them. That was *your* job." Darlene grabs a box and scrawls "flea market" on its side.

Lucy had forgotten that the task of cleaning the sitting room always fell to her for some misbehavior or other. Her sister, Miss Perfect, didn't get a punishment the entire summer. Miss Perfect got a tan and earned a lifesaving badge. Miss Perfect. That was the summer she gave that name to Darlene. She smiles to think of how it stuck to her sister throughout high school.

Darlene tosses the box to her. "I'll be upstairs," Darlene says. "If you need more boxes, there are extras in the back room."

Lucy turns the glass elephant between her fingers. "Each figurine has a story," Aunt Lydia had said, and she told the stories to Lucy: How the elephant worked for a circus and helped put up the big top. How the duck was mother to ten ducklings and walked them from the pond to the ocean and back each day. How the dog led a blind woman all through Cape May on her errands. How the bear protected her cubs from the tiger.

Even as an eleven-year-old, Lucy had known that bears and tigers didn't live in the same environment, but she didn't contradict Aunt Lydia. She just watched with interest as her aunt placed the glass animals into story groups. She wonders now whether she had kept her silence out of respect or because she was afraid that Aunt Lydia would stop telling the stories and would ignore her like everyone else did.

"No time for pity parties. Leave those woe-is-me moments for Darlene; she's so good at them," Lucy mutters, moving on to another glass figurine.

She looks inside the box her sister had tossed at her. No newspapers. Nothing in which to wrap the tiny statues. "Hey, Miss Perfect! Where's the paper?" she yells to the ceiling.

"What paper?" her sister's voice calls down from one of the bedrooms.

"You know. To protect the glass animals."

"Lucy, they're just going to a flea market. The most we'll get is fifty cents a piece for them, scratches, nicks, and all."

"Aunt Lydia wouldn't like that."

"Aunt Lydia is dead."

The words sting Lucy's heart. Aunt Lydia is dead. Aunt Lydia's life is being sent to a flea market. Aunt Lydia's house is going to be sold. Aunt Lydia is about to disappear.

She gathers all the figurines from the shelf, tucking them into a fold of her T-shirt and carrying them to the mahogany coffee table. Sitting on the brocade claw-foot settee, she arranges them into one of the stories she remembers Aunt Lydia telling her. The story is about how the squirrel taught all the other animals to prepare for the winter by storing food. Aunt Lydia's stories never made any scientific sense, but they always had a good moral.

"Mommy!" Darlene's five-year-old twins burst into the room and immediately spot the tiny glass animals. "I wanna play," Cindy says, climbing up on the sofa next to Lucy.

"Me, too," her sister Mindy adds, reaching for the glass duck.

Darlene dresses the twins alike. Lucy thinks they look like porcelain dolls, always pretty, never dirty. Like their mom, even in that, she thinks.

"You have to be very careful," she warns them. "They're not toys. They break easily."

The two girls lift and examine each of the figurines, exaggerating their careful handling of the tiny glass animals.

Lucy had gotten pregnant once but wasn't ready then to end the party-of-a-life she had with Hank. Now, she has a case of the what-ifs. What if she had carried that pregnancy to term? What would the child have been like? Would it have been pretty and smart like Darleen's kids? Or would it have come into this world damaged?

She thinks about Hank and the life they shared in that fourth-floor walk-up on Ninth Avenue. She remembers the kinds of friends they had, the booze, the drugs. Yeah, she was right in ending her pregnancy. That kid would have been taken from her anyway and she would have just put the child into the same kind of crappy life she'd mapped for herself. Yeah, she'd made the right decision. And she'd made a few more right decisions: to leave Hank, to sober up, to start over. She touches her leather bracelet with its dangling silver "A." She wears it as a reminder of her daily struggle against alcoholism.

The twins whisper to each other and move the glass animals along the table, changing the groupings. Lucy guesses they're creating their own stories. She and Darlene never did anything like that when they were little; she could only remember fights and tears and wishing she were an only child.

Cindy and Mindy look up from the coffee table and smile their mother's smile. The pageant smile, Lucy used to call it. Until then, she had considered telling the twins Aunt Lydia's stories, but they look so much like miniature Darlenes that she can't bring herself to share her great-aunt with them. Instead, Lucy turns to the task of boxing books from Aunt Lydia's bookcases, a task that requires no tissue paper or newspapers, a task that will go quickly because she has no interest in her great-aunt's large collection of paperback romance novels and the faux-leather-bound hardback set of classic literature titles that were bought in monthly installments.

She kneels in front of the bookcase and starts packing the books by type and size, not bothering to read the titles, until one stands out—a rather large faded hardback with a watercolor fairy on its cover. *The Blue Fairy Book*. It was the book Aunt Lydia had brought to the third-floor guest room the night Darlene went to Sandy Larson's slumber party at the Cape May Country Club.

> When Aunt Lydia opened the front door, Mrs. Larson and Sandy were standing there, beautiful-people smiles on their faces.
>
> "The girls are going to have a great time,"

Mrs. Larson said.

Sandy grabbed Darlene's overnight bag and the two friends ran to the car, laughing.

"Thanks, Aunt Lydia," Darlene called back.

It was as though Lucy were invisible. She rushed up the stairs and flung herself across the quilt. After the sound of the car leaving, she listened for the footsteps of her great-aunt. As the sound got nearer, she turned her back to the door and pretended she was sleeping.

Aunt Lydia sat on the side of the bed and rubbed Lucy's shoulder. "We'll read some stories, okay?" Then her aunt noticed the cut on her niece's forearm. "Lucy? How did this happen?"

Lucy didn't tell her that she did it to herself, that she took the broken seashell and dug hard into the skin, or that she did this whenever she got angry or sad, and sometimes for no reason whatsoever. She didn't want Aunt Lydia asking more questions, questions that she didn't have answers for or just didn't want to think about. Instead, she made up a story about tripping over a blanket at the beach.

Lucy didn't know if her aunt believed her, but nothing was said of it after that night. Aunt Lydia gave her the book. The rest of the summer, she passed the hours by sitting in the window seat, reading the stories, on sunny days as well as rainy. She was content. She created her own world with Aunt Lydia's help.

That had been her first journey into escape. Later, there would be boys and sex and weed and booze. Though she attends the weekly AA meetings, Lucy still feels the craving for one tiny drink, just enough to dull the pain. She pinches the skin on her wrist and holds it until the feeling passes. Then she sits on the floral carpet and pages through the book. She wonders why it was left behind, why she hadn't taken it with her when her mother returned to Cape May to collect her and Darlene and cart them back to their home in Philadelphia.

She had forgotten the beauty of the illustrations in the book. Each illustration pulls her imagination into a new world, a world without sisters or nieces or estates or divorce or loneliness. She feels as though she's being lifted into the sky, the breeze moving through her hair, the clouds surrounding her. She's on a magic carpet with a dark-haired prince. She's ...

"Lucy!"

Boom. Back to earth.

Darlene is standing over her, arms folded, giving her a parental look of disapproval. "We've got to get this done today."

"Why?" Lucy asks, standing up to Darlene, hugging the book against her chest, her index finger keeping the page marked. "Why does it all have to be done today? Why does it have to be done at all?"

"So we can get it over with and move on with our own lives. So I can finish the estate papers. So we can sell this place. Surely, you can use the cash." Her sister places an extra box by the settee. "Girls, help Mommy. Put the glass animals in the box, okay?"

Lucy drops the book on the floor and rushes to the coffee table with her hands spread open. "Don't!" she shouts.

Cindy and Mindy look from their mother to Lucy and back again.

"Girls, go outside and play on the glider. The adults have to talk." After the girls leave, Darlene continues. "Lucy, stop getting in the way. You don't have the estate on your shoulders like I do. As always, I have to be the responsible one."

"But you're treating everything like it's junk."

"It is. It is junk. There's nothing of value except some of Aunt Lydia's jewelry. We'll split those pieces if you want something to remember her by. There's a pearl necklace, an emerald ring, and a pair of ruby earrings. The rest is just cheap costume jewelry. I was going to give it to the girls to play with, but, if you want any of it, it's yours."

"How can you be so cavalier about Aunt Lydia's things?"

"That's it, Lucy, they're just things. I can't get maudlin over every spoon and fork. There's no time for that. I need to get the house on the market."

"Why can't we just keep the house?"

Darlene looks at her as though she's dealing with an imbecile. "I didn't realize you'd become a millionaire. How did I miss that?"

"Very funny, Darlene."

"I'm not being funny. It's what this house is worth. Being close to the ocean makes it very valuable. It'll go for a million or more. Enough for my girls to go to college. Enough for Michael and me to get out of our crowded brownstone. Enough to pay off our credit card debt," she said, "And enough for you to get your own life together. It's about time, too." Darlene delivers the knock-out punch. "About time you grow up and stop asking the world to love you."

"Love me?"

"Yes, love you. Poor Lucy. Long-suffering Lucy. Lucy, who Aunt Lydia doted on. Lucy, who went off to boarding school."

"Boarding school? Darlene, it was a prison for bad girls, didn't you get that?"

"And it cost Mom a lot of money to send you there. So much money that I couldn't take piano lessons anymore," she says. "You owe me, Lucy. And Aunt Lydia has given us the money that finally pays me back."

"Pays you back? For that summer of your glorious conquests? The swimming? The parties? The trips? While I stayed behind with Aunt Lydia? While I cleaned the house? While I read books and kept out of everyone's way?"

"You mean, while Aunt Lydia fawned all over you, and let you play with her precious glass animal collection, and gave you the best room—the one on the top floor?" Darlene's face reddens. "I'd have given anything for the attention you got."

"Attention? You thought it was attention?"

"Of course it was. You were the baby. You were the needy one," Darlene says. "And I had to be the independent one. I had to take care of myself. I had to do everything right so Momma would only have to worry about you."

"She should have worried about herself."

Darlene moves to the settee. "Momma had a tough life."

"She brought it on herself, Darlene. If she hadn't gotten involved with Steve, her life might have been fine."

"And you and I would never have been born."

Lucy shrugs. "So what?"

"The twins would never have been born, either. I can't bear to imagine that."

"I wouldn't miss anything. Certainly not the years I wasted with Hank or the shitty job I have."

"You wouldn't miss *anything*?"

Lucy shrugs. "Maybe Aunt Lydia. She was the best part of my life." She sits on the floor, the coffee table barricading her from her sister. "I used to dream of coming back here to Cape May and taking care of Aunt Lydia. I thought I would finally be home." She feels her face flush as regret rushes over her. "I know what you're thinking. I waited too long, and now Aunt Lydia is dead."

Suddenly, Darlene reaches across the table and grabs her hand. "No. I wasn't thinking that at all." Then, just as quickly, she releases her hand as though the grab has surprised her, too. She fills the silence with, "Life gets so busy and complicated, and the next thing you know, we've missed out."

Lucy nods. Her sister's words seem trite, but Lucy appreciates them for what they are—an effort to console her. She wishes that she and Darlene had more practice in talking honestly to one another.

"Lucy, you must know we can't keep this house. I'm sorry. Really, I am," her sister whispers, as though it's too difficult to voice the words. "If you want, you can keep the glass animals. Aunt Lydia would give them to you if she were here." She holds out the glass elephant.

Lucy accepts the elephant and cradles it in the palm of her hand. With the dust cleared from its surface, the glass catches the light, shining like a diamond in the morning sun. This is all she had needed from her older sister—recognition of the special importance of Aunt Lydia and respect for what this house means to her.

A memory stirs and, with it, a decision. "Come with me," she says to Darlene. "I want to show you something." She takes her sister up to the third-floor bedroom, to a door in the back wall of the closet, to a staircase that leads to a ceiling door. When Lucy opens the latch, sunshine spills though the opening. "It's the crown of the house," she tells her sister.

The two women stand on the small platform at the highest point of the roof, a space enclosed by a white decorative railing. All those years ago, Darlene had pointed to the roof and called it the crown of the house, but only Lucy knew its real name and its reason for existing.

It was the night that Darlene was invited to watch the Cape May Fourth of July fireworks from a boat on the Delaware Bay. Lucy was broken-hearted that she was not invited to tag along.

Aunt Lydia sat on the bed with Lucy. "I know what will cheer you up." She opened the closet door and

slid the hanging clothing to the side; then she
pulled away a bed sheet that had been tacked to the
back wall. "Look," she said, revealing the door that
opened to a staircase.

Lucy watched her great-aunt climb up the stairs
and push open a roof hatch, letting moonlight fill the
staircase. "This will be our secret."

Aunt Lydia told her that this special spot was called
a "widow's walk" and that is was meant to provide a
perch for a fisherman's wife to search the sea for her
husband's boat when it was overdue.

That night, she and her great aunt watched the fireworks from
the roof, and for the rest of the summer, Lucy sneaked up to the
widow's walk each night to look at the stars and dream. Maybe
her sister is right; maybe Lucy was the recipient of the best gifts
that summer in Cape May. The stories. The top-floor bedroom.
The widow's walk. Aunt Lydia's attention.

"I'm sorry, Darlene. Really. I never realized that you were as
lost as I was. You always seemed so together and confident."

"Seemed," Darlene repeats. "Just seemed."

Darlene looks out over the town to the beach and the families
gathered there. "It's a beautiful view," she says, turning in a circle
to see each part of Cape May.

The sound of giggling comes from the front porch, where the
twins are playing on the old metal glider. "I wish we could have
been close like they are," Lucy says.

Darlene sighs. "Momma should have done better for us. She
shouldn't have let the wedge between us get so far."

"Momma was broken. Let's not allow that to keep us broken,
too."

Darlene nods. "If we treat each other the way you cared for
Aunt Lydia's glass figurines, we might be okay."

Lucy imagines Darlene with her in scenes that never happened—the two of them moving the glass animals around a table while Aunt Lydia told a story, and she and her sister sitting together in the window seat while their aunt read from *The Blue Fairy Book*. Without effort, the words of one special tale come to mind, and Lucy says them aloud as though she has no control over the telling. "A poor widow had two children. One was called Snow-White and the other Rose-Red, and they were the sweetest and best children in the world, always obedient and always cheerful. The two children loved each other so dearly that they always walked about hand in hand whenever they went out together, and when Snow-White said, 'We will never desert each other,' Rose-Red answered: 'No, not as long as we live.'"

For the first time in forever, Lucy feels a twinge of sisterly affection. She holds out her hand, and Darlene accepts it. Strange, it seems, but she has no doubt that somehow her aunt is responsible for this. She smiles at Darlene. "Aunt Lydia would have loved for this to be her legacy."

Why You Trashed Vera Wang

You wish that you'd kept that Keurig coffeemaker you got as a wedding present, but since it came from Josh's sister, it seemed only right to give it back. No wedding, no Keurig. But after consuming so much alcohol last night, you're desperate for caffeine to lighten the pounding headache.

Consider walking six long blocks to Starbucks, but change your mind to avoid running into straggler wedding guests who haven't left Rehoboth yet. You couldn't bear the awkward smiles and pretending that everything is fine. Look in the cabinet above the sink at the beach cottage and find an old Mr. Coffee and an opened tin of Maxwell House. Say, "Desperate times call for desperate measures," and brew what you've got. Fill the "I Love Dolphins" mug and sip. Stale. Cry out, "Why me?" like Nancy Kerrigan when the baseball bat struck her leg. Accuse the universe of being unfair. Reach into the pink canvas "I'm the Bride" tote, pull out an almost-empty bottle of Godiva Chocolate Vodka from last night's pity party, and wish that you'd accepted your maid of honor's offer to stay at the "honeymoon" cottage with you. Pour half the cup of flat coffee down the drain to make room for the liquor, while telling yourself that chocolate vodka can fix anything.

Carry the mug to the front porch and settle into one of the battered wicker rockers. The cushion is lumpy but soft. You think of big butts sitting on these faded blue and white stripes and start singing the lyrics of the Queen song "Fat Bottomed Girls," until you realize that the old man walking his Yorkie can hear you.

Start the refrain again. There's no reason to blush or be embarrassed; nothing can match the humiliation you felt yesterday morning when Josh didn't show up at St. Edmond's Church and the priest had to announce to the guests that there would be no wedding but that everyone was still invited to partake of a lovely lunch at the Rehoboth Beach Country Club.

You watch the old man and his Yorkie disappear down the street and wish you had a dog. Dogs are faithful and affectionate. They don't fake their feelings; their kisses are honest kisses. Sure, a dog might accidentally pee on your Oriental rug, but that's not done in full view of your entire family and all your friends on what's supposed to be the most important day of your life. Yeah, you need a dog.

And you need a better chair cushion. Try all six rockers on the porch, and acknowledge that you're a Goldilocks who never finds the "right" one of anything. Shelve that thought and replace it with the question of how many summer guests' behinds squished the cotton stuffing of these cushions into uneven mounds. Make up a number and say, "1,749" as though it were the answer. Laugh at the silliness of it all. Relish the way the laugh feels. On your mouth. Across your cheeks. In your heart.

You thought you'd never laugh again. You were wrong. You were wrong about a lot of things.

Decide that life is too short for bad coffee, even when it's doctored by vodka. Toss the rest of the drink over the railing, aiming for the grass but, due to your lack of athletic skill, showering the edge of the garden. Watch as brown liquid drips from the white of the daisies like muddy gutter rain splashed on a bridal gown. Resolve to hate the color white, sterile as sheets in a hospital, lifeless as an empty promise.

Energized by your decision, rush into the house and up the stairs to the second floor, discarding your T-shirt and untying the string of your gray jersey-knit yoga pants. Drop these to the floor of the bedroom and dig through the partly unpacked suitcase to find your new floral bikini, with its vibrant reds and yellows. Hold it in the air to admire.

You catch a glimpse of your naked body in the antique mirror. Stop everything. Study the shape of your rounded hips and perky breasts. The mirror says that Josh is missing out on something wonderful. You think this may be the best you've ever looked. Blushing at your brazen admiration of your own body, pull on the bikini and tie a sarong around your waist.

You look good. Fashion-model good. And ready for a swim. Of course the beach will be crowded with July beachgoers. Strategize. Weigh the advantages and disadvantages of squeezing into a spot in the center of the dense forest of beach umbrellas versus taking a chance on plopping by the water's edge. Like shopping real estate, choosing the right spot on the beach is an important decision. You become overwhelmed by the question, *Do I want to disappear, or do I want to be noticed?* You don't have an answer. Until yesterday, you were half of the "Josh & Marcy invite you to a wedding" couple. Now, you're solo. Single. Available. And your brain is a wobbling plate of Jell-O.

Suddenly, you feel stuck, unable to move from the room. The friendly mirror turns against you and becomes a funhouse mirror, distorting your body, revealing every part of you that you hate. Every pound you lost for the wedding seems to have returned and doubled in the flash of a moment of doubt. Decide that the bikini is too skimpy and maybe too desperate. Toss the sarong over the suitcase, pull on the yoga pants, and retrieve your T-shirt. You still look fat. Undesirable. Left at the altar.

Pop open a bottle of champagne lifted from the reception lunch and return to the porch with the opened bottle in hand like a skid row drunk with expensive taste. Sip champagne directly from the bottle, and rock the wicker rocker back and forth, back and forth. Listen to the rhythmic complaint of the uneven wood boards of the porch as each forward and each backward carries the sound of wood against wood. Accept the thud-thud of the rocker against the boards as proof of the unevenness of your life.

Take another sip of champagne and replay the past year. All the wedding details: contracts (sip), designs (sip), tastings (sip), deposits (sip), and, most frustrating of all, the endless search for the perfect gown, the one that would bring the tears that every bride is supposed to experience when finding it. Take a double sip of champagne because you never had those tears, and that should have been enough warning that something was wrong with the wedding. Yet you still handed the bridal shop your credit card for the $7,000 Vera Wang gown.

Stomp up the stairs, swinging the champagne bottle. Open the closet door and toast the billowy organza skirting of the gown and the tulle-draped bodice with its sweetheart neckline. Consider the possibility of selling it on eBay, but reject the idea because you don't want anyone else to be the first person to walk down the aisle in this gown. You'd rather see it ripped to shreds and dragged from the back of your car all the way home to Washington, DC, than see some other bride walk in this Vera Wang.

Twisting like a contortionist, you manage to get yourself dressed in the wedding gown without the help of bridesmaids. When you look into the mirror again, you see a bride looking back at you. Watch the tears slide down your face. Crap. *Now* you have the tears.

You can't take the gown off, not just because it's so difficult to reach the back buttons and you already wore out your arms getting into it, but also because you were meant to wear this gown. Consider becoming the jilted Miss Havisham from the Dickens novel you read in tenth grade, sitting in your wedding gown day after day until death, becoming the neighborhood eccentric. Reject that idea for a better one.

Walk barefoot in your $7,000 Vera Wang gown down Lake Avenue to the beach, ignoring the occasional pinch of a sharp stone or the snag of the skirt on a tree root. Weave through the maze of umbrellas and blankets that crowd the sand, aware of the accumulation of stares all around you. At the edge of the water, feel the ocean breeze flutter the layers of organza like flower petals in April. Inch your toes into the chilly water, take a breath, and run into the ocean, skirt lifted to catch each wave. Ignore the lifeguard's whistle. Let the waves knock you down. Then stand up and let them knock you down again. Repeat until the fabric of the skirt gets heavy with saltwater and begins to weigh you down. (Later, you'll compare yourself to Shakespeare's Ophelia, insane from being dumped by Hamlet, drowning in the river, dying from unrequited love, violins in the background.)

A lifeguard grabs your arm and pulls you to your feet. "What are you doing?"

Tell him, "Obviously, I'm trashing the dress."

A crowd on the beach cheers as you emerge from the water. You see someone taking your photograph with a cell phone and ask her to send you a copy to memorialize this event. She asks you why you trashed your wedding gown. Say, "It maxed out my Visa. It had to be punished." Laughing, she pushes the send button, and your image flies through space to its destination.

You're grateful that the beach patrol doesn't arrest you. Luckily, the soaked wedding gown hides the wobble of too much alcohol.

Walk back to the cottage in the sopping gown, a one-woman parade, smiling and waving like the celebrity you have just become. Think about starting a blog for jilted brides, preaching the therapeutic value of the popular new bridal tradition of "trashing the dress," only now applied to those left at the altar. When life gives you lemons, make a Long Island Iced Tea, right?

Outside the bedroom door, grab both sides of the bodice of

the Vera Wang and tug until the back buttons pop off, and then let the gown drop to the floor. Emerge like Botticelli's *Venus* from the clamshell. In the calm pastel blue of the bedroom, climb under the covers of the bed. Exhale. Feel released from the baggage of regret, and fall asleep in mid-thought.

Shifting Sands

Stormy Skies

The Gypsy Heart

J enny's chest labored at each breath as she fiercely pedaled the pink bicycle down the beach road leading to the state park. She was unaccustomed to exercise; however, only a cyclist or a pedestrian could bypass the locked security gate at the Gordon Pond entrance, and though she wanted another cigarette badly, there could be no time for stopping if she were to enter the park before the arrival of early morning fishermen. Her mission on this September morning was best performed without witnesses.

She held tight to the handlebars. She'd not ridden this bicycle for so long that she had to pump its flat tires when she took it from the shed. She hoped the air would last until she reached her destination, and she worried about the gravel that caught the tires and bounced her like an off-balanced washing machine, causing the object she carried in her windbreaker pocket to bump-bump, bump-bump against her, like a second heartbeat seeking syncopation with her own.

The thin light of pre-dawn gave the world the look of a black-and-white photograph disturbed only by the pink of Jenny's bicycle. In the early morning mist, a gauze of pale gray covered the pastels of the beach houses. Any other day, she would have played pick-the-house-of-your-dreams on her way to the park, imagining life in these elaborate McMansions, but today had its own focus. Suddenly, a rock snagged her front wheel and nearly sent her flying into a mailbox. She wobbled the bike straight again, then came to a standstill just outside the gated park entrance. She took a long breath. Automatically, she reached for her cigarettes, but stopped. No time, she thought. Not with the sun just starting to redden the sky.

She walked her bicycle around the gate, and then pedaled though the vacant parking lot to its farthest end. She felt tiny in the midst of so much emptiness. Solitary. The only other movement was the sway of the sea grasses that bordered the lots, like black ink lines on a watercolor. Jenny slid the front wheel of the bike into the metal stand near the path to the beach, unzipped the pocket of her windbreaker, and brought out the purple velvet pouch that had bounced against her chest during the uneven ride.

Loosening the drawstring of the bag, she removed a silver sweetheart locket. When she was sixteen, she thought it was so beautiful—two roses, their stems entwined, surrounded by a circle of leaves. Late at night, she would sit by her bedroom window and tilt the locket in the moonlight to watch the sparkles dance around those lines. Back then she kept it hidden, tucked in an unmatched gym sock in the bottom drawer of her dresser. It was a secret she shared with no one, not even her best friend Kathleen.

Jenny had gone alone to see the gypsy woman. She had taken the fifty dollars she'd earned from working extra hours at the DQ. In her youthful imagination, a magical charm was the only way, she thought, to bring her true love David back to her and end the unbearable silence of their breakup. Her fifty dollars bought the promise that this locket, with its miniscule photographs of David and her, would produce that spell. The gypsy assured her that, when completed, "It will bring him back to you." It seemed so silly now, even sillier considering that, although she hadn't finished the last part of the spell, David had asked her to the prom that year and they had dated again until late August, when he left for college in Virginia. She remembered contemplating the charm a few times while David was away at school, and later, after he moved to Texas with a new job and a fiancé he'd gained along the way, but she'd never sent the locket into the ocean to complete the gypsy's spell. Instead, she placed the devalued locket into a Nike shoe box with other memories of high school: her JV letter for basketball, a dried-up wrist corsage, streamers from spirit day assemblies, and numerous photographs, including one class picture with two small holes where faces had been removed.

Clutching the miniature silver heart in her fist, she marched past the sea grass to the beach, determined to finish now what she had not finished twenty years ago; she would bring David back to her. Her brisk walk slowed as the cool sand of dawn grabbed at her feet and pulled them into the tiny dunes each footstep made. Annoyed, she kicked off her sandals. Her task was to be done quickly and with finality. If she had time to think, perhaps she would question the morality of this action. Or its logic. She would wonder if a charm cast so many years ago would still be potent, and whether the gypsy's words "bring him back to you" could mean that literally.

Reaching the jetty, she began the hopscotch dance toward the farthest rock, the one that received each wave on its outer edge. *Damn.* A sharp spot caught her left foot. Balancing on the other, she inspected the trickle of blood that was already sliding down her arch. As a kid, she'd climbed and jumped these rocks so many times that she should have known better than to remove those sandals. *Double damn.* There was no time to stop for this. She continued her journey, not caring that she left behind a trail of fresh red splotches.

She reached the head rock and fought for her balance. This rock had been an important part of her high school life. In ninth grade, she had been dared to stand on this rock during a nor'easter and had faced down the walls of violent waves the storm threw at her. Jenny's friends, who had gathered at the grass line to see if she would chicken out, declared her the queen, and

David named this rock "Queen's Throne." Afterward, she and David would skip classes to sit on Queen's Throne and look out over the ocean. Here, some promises were made that never came to be.

The waves this morning weren't the gigantic walls of water she had faced that day. Yet even in the calm of this September morning, she knew that a wave could toss a careless someone into the rocks. Living near this beach all her life, she'd heard of it often. The slip. The fall. The blood. Sometimes, the drowning, if no one were nearby to help. Death.

Last night, death came as a pickpocket hovering behind his unsuspecting victim and stealing away with the precious gem. When the phone rang after 10 p.m., Jenny knew it could not be a hello-how-are-you-doing call. Even when the caller ID displayed the name of her old friend Kathleen, now living on the West Coast with its different time zone, her heart anticipated the burden of bad news.

"David's gone."

There were details, but Jenny couldn't remember anything but those two words. She stayed up the whole night, smoked a pack of cigarettes, and drank a large portion of Southern Comfort because it had been David's favorite liquor. She had sat on the living room floor, lifting the contents from the Nike box, placing each item on the floor before her. She spent time with each piece, telling herself the stories of each of them—stories that always led back to David. She took her time with every memory and made herself wait until the box was empty of all but the velvet pouch. Finally touching the bag, Jenny felt the energy of the sixteen-year-old who had brought the locket home with such hopes. Awake still at 5 a.m., the decision to complete the gypsy's spell seemed reasonable.

This was the time to learn if the charm could "bring him back to you" as the gypsy had promised. Opening her hand, she unfastened the locket's clasp and looked at the faces of the two teenagers. They looked so much younger than she had remembered. He wore his hair long. She had acne. Jenny recalled that she'd "borrowed" the photographs from a group picture in a folder at the yearbook office. That had been another of her risky escapades in youth. She wondered what happened to that brave, spunky girl. When had her life become ordinary?

She heard the sound of a car and closed the locket tight. Time was moving too fast for remembrances. The sun was a half circle on the horizon, and the park was opening. She stood tall, back stretched toward the sky, and flung the locket far out from the jetty. She saw it plunk into a distant wave, and then flip up into the air, tossed wave to wave like a game of catch. She kept her eyes on the ocean's movement, hoping that the silver dot she saw was truly the locket and not the rays of the sun as it cleared the horizon.

When a seagull dipped toward the water and flew up again, Jenny lost sight of the silver heart. Had the seagull taken it? Damn it, she thought. Did that seagull take the locket? The charm would be ruined. How could David "come back to you" if there was no finish to the gypsy's spell?

Her anger swelled. She wanted to kill that bird. She wanted to beat its stupid head into the jetty rocks. Her hands tightened into fists, but it was useless. The seagull was already too far from shore and flying out farther across the ocean waves.

She sat on the rock and let its cold wetness seep through the back of her jeans; she didn't care. The locket was gone. David was gone. He was only thirty-six. Her age. Her first love. Her past. She took a cigarette from the dampened pack, expertly lit it, despite the wet and the wind, and drew in its smoky comfort. Around her, the beach was coming to life. Two fishermen were setting up their chairs to her left. A school of dolphins were leaping their way south. The sandpipers were skittering along the edge of the beach. Nothing changed. A charm tossed into the water, and nothing changed. What had she expected, anyway? Had she believed that David would rise from the water like a Greek god emerging from Poseidon's palace? That was a silly wish—a girl's wish. Death wasn't a fairytale where she, the princess, could kiss the prince awake.

The spray from the waves settled on her face and cooled the heat of her exertion. Jenny sighed. Fairy tale or not, she had expected a happy ending.

Her foot was throbbing. Searching in her windbreaker for a tissue to wipe away the blood, she found only the velvet bag. It would have to do. Once she had swabbed away the blood she could see the two curved lines of the cut. The shape reminded her of something. What was it? Then she recalled. The doodles she'd drawn on her notebooks in high school. It was the double curve she had made to indicate a seagull.

Maybe it was the lack of sleep. Maybe it was a need far down in her soul. But later, she would swear that this was a sign. There was no logic in a bird swallowing a metal locket, but what if that seagull were carrying David away, lifting him from the earth of dust and taking him up into the clouds and away? And, if it were, couldn't that be the magic?

Stormy Skies

Without Warning

An elephant in the sky. That's how Celia saw the gray cloud moving overhead. Of all things to imagine, she saw an elephant in the sky. It made her want to laugh. Maybe she was thinking about the metaphor "an elephant in the room." That would be her upcoming divorce from Sam, an event that had been looming over her for almost a year, an event that brought her to Rehoboth to "think things out." She snuggled into the sling canvas of the beach chair, setting time and distance from the chess match being played out between her lawyer and Sam's. In this moment, on this beach, she had all that she needed: a juicy romance novel, just enough sun between the rolling clouds, and time with her five-year-old twins, who were busily rearranging the sand with their plastic shovels. She breathed in the salty air, closed her eyes for a moment, and quickly fell into a light sleep, the kind of sleep that only mothers know, a sleep that is half restive and half alert, on the ready to protect her little ones.

Her mind drifted into dreams that were crazy, filled with odd disjointed moments—locked doors, a broken elevator, a pile of mismatched socks—a collage of irritating situations. But the mild annoyance of those moments dropped away and her imagination moved to a terrifying dream of her children being taken away in an ice cream truck while a neighbor's irrigation system sent water spraying over her. She knew she was dreaming, but she wouldn't leave that dream until she could rescue her children, who were screaming "Mommy! Mommy!" from the truck.

Something touched her arm, and she jolted awake.

"Mommy! Mommy!"

She was relieved to see that it was her daughter Emma, tapping her and waving a princess doll in front of her.

"Very pretty," she said to her daughter.

The cloudy sky had turned gray, and a few scattered raindrops were falling. Not enough to stop Ethan from digging faster to finish his castle or to get Emma to put away her doll.

Celia smiled. Wouldn't it be great to be a kid again, with no problems, unaffected by this sudden rain, totally focused on imaginary worlds? She gathered her book and her iPod into her beach bag, then leaned back into her chair and let the irregular drops of rain splash against her skin. It's only water. And they were all in their swimsuits anyway.

But suddenly the wind picked up. A yellow beach umbrella nearby was uprooted from the sand like a dandelion ripped from a garden, and Celia grabbed the end of her own umbrella to prevent it from escaping as well. Before the gusts of wind could turn the umbrella inside out, she closed its metal arms and shoved the umbrella into its plastic storage sleeve.

"I think we'd better pack up your toys and leave before …"

On cue, random heavy drops of rain began to fall, and the shrill sound of lifeguard whistles blasted the air. A crackle of thunder was followed by another blast from the lifeguard whistle as the young lifeguard stood on his guard chair and waved his arms toward the boardwalk.

Celia sighed. Weather. Just one more thing in her life over which she had no control. Like whether or not the divorce decree will give her primary custody of the twins, or whether she'll get alimony as well as child support, or whether her soon-to-be ex-husband Sam will get to simply walk away, leaving her to find a paralegal position somewhere and pick up where she left off in her career before pregnancy and motherhood put her professional goals on hold.

Another clap of thunder, this time louder, and a now-serious wind spurred the beachgoers to give in to the inevitable, sending couples and families scurrying from the beach. "Come on, guys," Celia said to her children. "We need to go back to the hotel until the storm passes over."

But a wind gust snatched a silver princess doll gown from Emma's hand and carried it down the beach. Celia grabbed her daughter before she could run after it. "I'll buy you another one."

Emma whined, "But that's my favorite."

Her twin brother stomped on this sandcastle and announced, "I'll get it!"

"No, you won't!" Celia said, reaching to grab the end of his T-shirt. But he was too quick and took off running in the direction of the silver gown's flight. "Ethan!" she shouted, "Come back here right now!" But her son was racing hard through the beach crowd, focused solely on the pursuit. "Damn! I don't need this right now," Celia muttered softly enough to keep her daughter from hearing the "D" word.

She lifted Emma. "Hold on tight to Mommy." With a quick glance to their belongings, Celia grabbed only the small canvas Browseabout Books tote that contained her wallet and hotel keys and began a wild zigzagging run down the beach, dividing her attention between searching for Ethan and avoiding collision with the fleeing beach crowd. "Ethan!" she screamed above the babble, as college kids from the rental shack rushed past them, chasing the bright blue rented umbrellas and carrying three or four piled high in their arms. Thunder boomed so loudly that it echoed in Celia's ears. Then, a quick flash of light, and the clouds burst with the punch of water balloons dropped from a balcony.

Balancing her daughter on one hip, Celia pushed back her rain-soaked hair and blinked at the almost-empty beach. Ethan was not there. Her mind raced to the news story she'd seen last week about a boy abducted in a city park in Wilmington, his body found two days later in a dumpster. She felt as though she'd been kicked in the stomach.

A lifeguard rushed up to her. "Miss, everybody's gotta leave the beach when there's lightning. It's the rule."

Celia exploded. "Don't you think I know that? Do you really think I'm still on this beach for the hell of it?" She struggled against the sob that rattled in her chest. "I'm sorry. It's just that my little boy is missing, and I can't find him."

The lifeguard looked around for assistance. "Let me take you to beach patrol HQ. You'll be safe there, and we can get the a police officer to look for your son."

"No," she said. "*I* need to do this. *I* need to find my son." She could just hear Sam telling the judge that she was an unfit mother and using this as evidence. That's just what he'd do so he could get full custody of their kids—anything to hurt her. That thought spurred Celia to move on. She trudged toward the boardwalk as the wind pummeled her with shards of rainwater that mixed with her Coppertone lotion, making her bare arms slick and her grip on Emma tenuous. She held her daughter tighter. She was determined that nothing and no one would take her children from her. Nothing and no one.

The boardwalk had cleared as everyone took shelter. Groups of families crammed under the canvas awnings of the stores, wrapped in colorful blankets and cover-ups, looking like circus performers under the big tent. Celia scanned the faces of the children who peeked between their parents to watch the lightning crisscross the sky. None of those faces belonged to her Ethan.

She felt her energy torn from her by the forceful wind that buffeted her face with strands of wet hair. Her daughter was crying "Mommy," but Celia couldn't do more than stand in her own silence. When the lifeguard brought a police officer, she let herself be led to patrol headquarters, a half block down the boardwalk. There, she gave a description of Ethan as she fumbled with her wallet for the emergency cards she had made during a Keep Your Child Safe program at the mall. "And he was wearing a Harry Potter T-shirt."

The officer called in the description to the others on duty and the search began, but Celia couldn't bear to sit still while strangers looked for her son. "I want to go, too."

Emma clung to her mother. "No, Mommy, no. Don't leave me."

The officer directed her to remain seated. "We need you to stay here with your daughter; we don't need to be adding a search for a missing mother." He introduced himself as either Eddie or Lenny. She wasn't sure which name, if either of them, was said. It wasn't important. All that mattered was finding her son Ethan, and never having to let the court system find out that she had lost him, even if it were only for a short time and under the unusual circumstances of a sudden storm. Officer Eddie/Lenny opened a note pad and started to write his report. Where were they staying? "The Tide's Inn, room 103." Were there any other family members at the hotel who should be told that she and her daughter were safe inside the station? "No. It's just the three of us." Was there a husband who should be contacted? "God, no." But Emma said, "Daddy," and then Celia had to explain that she and Daddy were in the throes of a divorce. Was there a chance that he had taken his son?

Celia panicked. Had Sam taken Ethan? She shook the idea from her head. "He doesn't know we're here." She saw the officer's eyebrows rise. "I mean, he knows we're at the beach. He just doesn't know which one. Or maybe he does. His lawyer's quite slick." Were there visitation issues? "He gets them one weekend each month. At least for now." She kissed Emma's forehead and leaned back into the chair to wait, frustrated at her inability to take action.

The lifeguard entered with a pile of items abandoned on the beach.

"That's Mommy's," Emma said, pointing to a Vera Bradley tote.

The iPod and other items inside the bag were insignificant to Celia in light of her missing child, but Emma took possession of her mommy's bag long enough to retrieve her Hello Kitty Beanie Baby.

The rain pounded against the station and sent a constant spray though the screen door, misting Celia's face. She watched a banner from the pizza shop dip and rise again with the wind in a magic-carpet dance. Over the ocean, bolts of lighting cascaded down the sky, accompanied by the steady drum of thunder. She shivered, partly from the chill of the ceiling fan, and partly from the adrenaline that spiked and dropped and spiked again within her, but mostly at the fear of how everything can change in an instant. What if Ethan were really gone? Another shiver. A lifeguard placed a blanket over Celia's shoulders, and she pulled it around her daughter Emma, holding her close.

She felt anchored to the bench, stuck in a limbo of not know-ing, passively listening to the sounds of the room. The static of the weather radio. The spirited laughter of the lifeguards who stood around waiting for the storm to pass. The click, click, click of the second hand on the wall clock. The incongruity of time as it raced ahead and stood still at the same time.

She began to rock Emma until she felt her daughter slip into a nap. She thought back to when the twins were fragile preemies and how she would sit in the special care unit, aching to hold them, waiting to take them home. Emma had been released first. Celia remembered the nights she had rocked Emma to sleep while looking out the bedroom window, longing for her son to come home, as though he were Peter Pan and would fly in through the window to her.

The screen door slammed open and a young man in a soggy Nick's Pizza shirt entered with a stack of pizzas for the lifeguards, "Nick sent these to thank you for driving so many paying customers into his restaurant."

The staff cheered, and Emma, half-asleep, asked, "Mommy, did they find Ethan?"

"Not yet, sweetie."

"Why didn't he just go to home base?" her daughter asked.

The simple question exploded inside Celia with a rush of hope. "We've got to get to the hotel," she told Officer Eddie/Lenny.

"It would be better if you stayed here. You shouldn't be alone while we're conducting our search, and we might need to contact you when we find your son. He could be injured or something."

Celia suspected that the "or something" referred to the possibility of the police finding a body rather than a son, like the officers in Wilmington who found the body of the dead boy stuffed into a dumpster. Officer Eddie/Lenny was wrong.

"You don't understand. We need to get to The Tide's Inn. It's *home base*." She didn't have time to explain the concept of home base to this man. She grabbed Emma's hand and rushed out into the horizontal rain. The Tide's Inn was their home base in Rehoboth. Ethan might be, *would be*, waiting for them at the hotel. She needed to get there. Now.

The officer followed at a respectful distance behind them. As long as he didn't try to stop them, Celia was satisfied with the arrangement. Blinking the rain from her eyes, she rushed down Baltimore Avenue, lifted her daughter across rushing rivers of drain water, and sprinted down First Street and around the corner to the steps of the hotel.

The steps were empty.

Celia felt as though part of her had been cut away. Perhaps the officer's fears about Ethan were correct. Perhaps something darker than a divorce decree had taken her son from her. Perhaps she had lost him forever, and would lose his sister Emma, too. Overcome, she sank onto the steps.

Emma sat beside her. "Don't be sad, Mommy."

Officer Eddie/Lenny got on his radio and asked for any news of the missing boy. Celia's heart dropped farther when the voice on the other end replied, "No. Nothing. We're checking the arcade right now, but so far, no sign of the kid."

The arcade was where Celia had promised to take her children tonight after dinner. They were going to play some Skee-Ball and try to win enough tickets to get the fuzzy purple dolphin that Ethan and Emma had already named "Fin."

Behind them, Celia heard the hotel door open. "Mrs. Thornton?"

She turned to see the hotel receptionist standing in the doorway. Beside her, a cocoon of white hotel towels dropped to the floor, and Ethan emerged. He rushed to his mother. "Mommy!"

"When I saw him standing on the sidewalk in the rain," the woman said, "I got concerned about him, being so young and with lightning so close, but he said he had to stand there because it was *home base*. I thought it was a game. But when I didn't see you nearby, I insisted he wait in the lobby."

Celia lifted her son into the air and held him so tightly that he protested. "Mommy, I did what you told me to do. I waited at home base. Where were you? I was worried."

She thought back to that Keep Your Child Safe program at the mall and how her five-year-olds had learned the lessons better than she had. Still, having enrolled them into that program showed that her parenting skills weren't so bad after all. She could handle this single-parent thing. She would stand strong when she faced Sam across the table in the courthouse in September. She didn't need the house or the best car or anything else that would be divided in the divorce decree. All she needed was this—her children, safe and with her. And she intended to keep it that way. No one and nothing would take her children from her. Not a sudden storm, and not Sam.

The rain stopped as suddenly as it had begun, and a bit of sun broke through the clouds. If only there were a rainbow, it would be a perfect Hallmark card moment, Celia thought, and the idea made her laugh. For the first time in months, Celia believed in the possibility of a happy ending.

Letting Go

Her hometown was slipping into the pockets of over-zealous developers. Her best friend Jerry was dying. And Shelly believed that if she tried hard enough, she could keep them both alive.

She had been at Jerry's house until midnight, and then awake until 3 a.m. trying unsuccessfully to finish an article for the *Cape Gazette* before her deadline. She felt strongly about the topic of overdevelopment of the beach towns along the coastline, and she hoped her article would motivate Rehoboth locals to attend a hearing about a proposed hotel and conference center. Shelly knew that she should drive to the newspaper office, but how could she? Jerry was barely hanging on, and she hadn't slept enough to write coherently. Her passion for the town had been depleted by her grieving over the inevitable.

Exhausted, she wandered toward the beach to one of the white benches that dotted the boardwalk like seagulls waiting for a handout. "Take a cleansing breath," Jerry would say. Shelly imagined him sitting by the water, legs entwined, gazing at the horizon, inhaling the salt air. She took a slow, deep breath and imagined herself as a solitary reed of sea grass, swaying in the ocean breeze, bending but unbroken, and she felt the muscles in her neck release.

The surf was gentle today. Undersized whitecaps slid onto the beach, and then disappeared in foam, like days that tumble away leaving only a few scattered details, fragmentary glimpses of memory. Shelly remembered that, when she was a little girl, she used to cup her hands together and try to capture a piece of the wave. If she cupped her hands now, could she capture a memory forever? A golden day last summer. The ferry to Cape May. Sitting on the deck with Jerry, both of them laughing as the slight tilt of the boat teased the wheelchair that was then so integral to his life. The bracelet of seashells that clicked against her watch like the sound of a fork against a china dessert plate. Crepes at that café by the beach. What was its name? Henry's! She mustn't forget. She mustn't forget any of it, not one detail.

Shelly clung to her memories like a toddler to a blanket. And so many of those memories, so many of those moments of warmth, were connected to the beach. It was the gift her dad gave her so many years ago. When she was little, he would bring her here after work. They had the whole beach to themselves, or so she remembered it. They would play games, and Mom would sit on the blanket and keep score.

Mom. She died when Shelly was ten. Her dad had said that mom was in Heaven with the angels like that holy card of the Blessed Virgin he kept in his Bible. Now, whenever she thought of her mom, she always saw that picture. When dad died, he became part of that same holy card. Mom and dad—together— surrounded by porcelain-skinned seraphs.

And now, Jerry. *Until death do us part.*

No. Jerry's still alive. She repeated it to herself several times to make sure that it was true. She erased his face from the card in her mind. There was still time to say the things that waited in her heart.

She walked back to Jerry's house and into the McDowell guest room at the end of the first-floor hallway. When the steps became a problem for him, Jerry had moved to this bedroom at the back of the house near the laundry room. "I love the smell of dryer sheets," he had claimed.

The door was open. The ceiling fan rotated air around the

Stormy Skies

room, causing the light curtains to breathe in and out from the window. Shelly observed how the sheet over Jerry's chest moved like the curtains. In. Out. In. Out. She crossed to a chair next to the bed by the tray of medicines that shouted to her brain, He isn't asleep! He's dying! In. Out. In. Out. It was the ventilator keeping the rhythm, not Jerry.

"Jerry," she whispered. "I wish …" What did she wish? That he'd open his eyes? That he'd sit up? That a cure would fall off some shelf in Heaven and land here on this bed?

Shelly gazed at him, the man she should have married. "I miss your voice," she said, and closed her eyes, coaxing her ears to remember his warm baritone sound.

"I knew you'd come back to me," rushed through her brain. But she knew it wasn't really his voice. Those were his words when he helped her move back home from New York three years ago, after her father died, back home to start over in the place she had so adamantly rejected at eighteen.

"I took a cleansing breath today," she said. "You would have been proud of me." She wished she could breathe that ocean air into his lungs, and make them expand with healing that would race through his body like a crusader, slashing away at the disease that was killing him. ALS. She and Jerry had made up so many meanings for those three letters. Their favorites were "Anticipate Loud Surf" and "Always Laugh Spontaneously." But nothing could alter the real meaning of those letters: Amyotrophic Lateral Sclerosis. Lou Gehrig's disease.

If anyone could escape this despicable disease, it would have been Jerry. He had taken up yoga and acupuncture and every type of New Age medicine that might coexist with what Dr. Garrison had prescribed, hoping that it might stave off his muscle degeneration, that it might prolong his life and their time together.

Jerry's sister Maggie stood in the doorway. "Dr. Garrison is on his way to check on Jerry. He said we can end this when we're ready."

"End it?" Shelly asked, but she knew what it meant. Dr. Garrison was suggesting the removal of life support, recommending that they let Jerry pass.

She saw the resignation in Maggie's eyes. "Shelly, we can't keep Jerry in this state of limbo forever. It isn't fair to him."

His sister was right. Jerry would stick around as long as she and Maggie needed. It was time to let him go. Shelly kissed his forehead and whispered, "Jerry, it's time for you to leave us. Maggie and I will be okay. We'll take care of each other. I promise."

While Maggie sang an old family lullaby to her brother, Shelly gazed at Jerry.

On wings of the wind o'er the dark rolling deep
Angels are coming to watch over thy sleep
Angels are coming to watch over thee
So list to the wind coming over the sea
Hear the wind blow, love, hear the wind blow ...

Before the end of the song, she knew that he was no longer there.

Outside the window, the sound of a tree crashing to the earth. The heavy machinery on the Anderson lot showed no respect for the passing of life that had just taken place in this back bedroom, no respect for the feelings of those gathered in this room. Shelly stepped back from the bed. Her mind photographed the room—scalloped curtains, papered walls, pine furniture, chenille spread—but not the medicines, the IVs, the ventilator. Later, she would add Jerry sitting by the window watching the Anderson kids play Frisbee where their house had once stood.

She wandered to the back porch and leaned her back against

the hardness of the Adirondack chair. Her mind was overwhelmed with "What now?" Call work to take a short leave of absence, enough time to help Maggie with the details, of course. And then? Sleepwalk through life for a while. Watch television too much. Read one of the dozens of dusty novels waiting in the corner of the living room. Meet her work deadlines. Learn to be alone again.

In the foreground, in the construction zone of the next lot, she watched the strangers busy themselves like ants full of purpose. One by one, this crew would fell the trees on the Anderson lot and then move on to constructing the new house. Home by home, business by business, the town would advance as surely as waves on an incoming tide.

She heard a car door close, but paid little attention to it. More than likely it was Dr. Garrison, and Maggie would take him back to her brother's room where he'd find that his patient had already passed away.

"Excuse me," a young man said as he approached the porch. "My wife and I are your new neighbors. Or, at least, we will be in a few months when the house is complete."

Shelly looked at the couple with some confusion. New neighbors?

"Do you mind if we take some pictures? We'd like to make a photo book of our house from its beginning." He was nodding toward the Anderson lot.

Finally, Shelly understood. "Of course." She would have explained that she didn't live here, but that would have led to her talking about Jerry and she didn't feel she was ready for that.

As the young man clicked his camera from a variety of positions in the McDowell back yard, his wife chattered away. "We're so excited. It's our first home. And I'm expecting," she said, pointing to her belly, although her pregnancy was barely showing. "This seems like a great town for raising children. And I love that our house is part of an older neighborhood. I love the feel of it. We wish that we could have just kept the original house, but there were so many plumbing and electrical issues, as well as a cracking foundation, that the only feasible option was to tear down and rebuild. But we've chosen a house plan that imitates the Craftsman period. We want to be respectful of the surrounding homes. You know, fit in."

They want to fit in, Shelly repeated in her mind. They want to respect the neighborhood. She took a deep breath and exhaled away the sense of despair that had held her captive for so many months. "New" doesn't have to mean "modern," nor does it have to erase the past. It just means moving onward. A huge weight lifted from her heart. What this couple brought with them was hope, and hope had been missing for too long. Shelly looked across the yard to a few of the older homes. They needed fresh paint. They needed new life. This neighborhood that had been filled with excitement and energy had become too somber in its old age, but young families like this could bring the laughter of children back to these streets.

"Do you like Frisbee?" Shelly asked.

The young woman looked confused. "Of course. Who doesn't like Frisbee?"

Shelly smiled. "Welcome to the neighborhood," she said, and meant it.

Starry
Nights

A Cougar at The Starboard

You know you shouldn't accept a third Tanqueray and tonic, but you're enjoying the attentions of this beachy lifeguard. Andy. Even his name is cute. So what if he's at least ten years younger than you—all the better that he doesn't seem to notice. You revel in feeling like a college girl, even though you're long past your sorority days. This is what you had hoped would happen on this weekend at the beach—this time away from the job hunt, the family responsibilities, and the monotony of monogamy, a.k.a. your marriage to Jack.

You only half-wish that Fran had stayed at The Starboard with you. Sure, this weekend wasn't so great so far, but this was supposed to be a reunion. Has it really been fourteen years since you and she were roommates at American University? You can't believe that time has rushed through your life as fast as your son Max used to tear down the hallway to escape a bath when he was a toddler. But fourteen years? You do the math. Max was born the winter after graduation, and he just turned thirteen in April. My God! Sometimes you forget, or at least try to forget, that you're the mother of a teenager.

You wish you hadn't thought of Max just now. What would your son think if he knew that Mom was weighing her morals vs. her needs? And at this moment, your needs are the larger of the two. You and Jack are "having problems," as the cliché goes. Jack's been distant, and you've been distant, and maybe the distance this weekend might be the cure. Or maybe not. At the very least, this weekend in Dewey will be a litmus test.

You hadn't heard from Fran in years, though you'd occasionally run into her mom at the mall: "Franchesca is doing so well … Franchesca got promoted to the international office … Franchesca is in Europe this month … Franchesca's Philadelphia home is being showcased in *Architectural Digest*." Okay, maybe you made up that last one, but your ultimate defense of "Really, Mrs. Whooton? Is Frannie still single?" ended her litany every time.

You laugh. Beach boy asks you what's funny. You tell him some crude joke that you heard Jack tell his brother last week—the one about the virgin, the farmer, and the horse. He can't hear the punch line over the music. You repeat it louder: "That's not my horse!" You both laugh.

There was a horse on the front of the Christmas card that Fran sent you this past December—the first card in years. Its postscript of "Miss you" opened the door between you again. When had that door closed, anyway? Was it your excursion into mommyhood or Fran's foray into the world of textiles? When had the birthday cards stopped and the last phone calls been made?

You were glad when Fran suggested a get-together for this May weekend at Dewey Beach, where you and she had spent that infamous week after graduation. That week when the Delta Gammas had the entire second floor of the Dewey Beach Motor Inn. That week of parties, and guys, and barhopping, and, for you, a magical night at The Starboard when a hunky fisherman showed you fireworks on the beach.

Beach boy puts his arm around your waist, drinks to your eyes. His are milk chocolate. So are his shoulders, which jut out beyond the frayed edge of his cotton shirt, the sleeves cut away just for this effect. Oh, to be eighteen again, you might wish, but really, you're glad to be past all those insecurities. Back then, you would have pictured yourself married to beach boy. Now, you just picture yourself naked with him. But it's just a game, and you're enjoying it.

When you had mentioned the reunion at the beach to your husband, he said, "You and Fran in Dewey again? Sure. Go. Have fun. Just remember that you're married, and stay away from The Starboard." So, if anyone is to blame for your spending this time with beach boy, it's Jack. "Stay away from The Starboard"? No effing way.

Beach boy leans over, nuzzles you behind the ear, and tells you that you're his kind of woman. You look around at the girls on the dance floor. Does that make me a brainless beach bunny? But you smile and tell him what he wants to hear—how handsome he is, how muscular his body is, how you just love a man who saves lives. A part of you hopes he'll save yours this evening, if having a wild night of crazy sex can perform that miracle. You blush at the boldness of this thought, and realize that the game is getting more dangerous than you'd planned. Are you really considering doing the dirty deed with this kid?

Beach boy Andy rubs your back in a circular motion. A "hmm" and almost a "yum" slides from your mouth. You can't remember the last time someone rubbed your back. Maybe your son, when he wanted you to buy him something ... or let him cheat on a curfew. You glance at the clock above the bar. It's nearly midnight. You wonder how long Jack is letting Max stay up watching videos. Quickly, you erase your mother face and replace it with the face of that "other woman" you're trying to be this weekend. You hope that beach boy will make a move soon. Before you chicken out. Before your makeup gets stale and lets those worry lines creep through. Before your tight black dress wilts, and you with it.

A busty cheerleader-type keeps brushing up against beach boy as she reaches for bar pretzels. You wonder if her boobs are real, or if, like you, she'll ever face the possibility of losing one of them. No, yours are originals with only a tiny biopsy scar on the left one, a reminder of how close you came last year to the disease that killed your mother. For a moment, you hate this girl. You hate that she's pretty and that she's young. You hate that she's the right age for beach boy. You hate yourself for sitting in this bar, pretending to be what you're not.

You never told Fran about that awful time when you feared breast cancer, and you don't want to think about it now, either. Think instead of the last time the two of you stayed in Dewey, the afternoon you sat in room 211, painting your nails pink like all the Delta Gammas, and planning how you'd live in France, meet important men and marry them, and become movers and shakers in the fashion industry. Those were great days.

It brings a smile to your face. Beach boy thinks the smile is for him. You don't tell him the truth. Why start now? "Are you having a good time?" he asks and laughs. It seems an odd question until you realize that you've been keeping time to the music with your hips and he's been enjoying the show. You work your hips some more, this time with a come-and-get-it wink. You think of *Sex and the City* and wonder if you're trying too hard.

"Having a good time. Wish you were here," echoes through your mind. It's what you and Fran had written on the postcards you sent each other as a joke during that last vacation together— free ones from the front desk—a photographic collage of the front of the motel, the pool, the inside of a room, the ocean, and the words "Dewey Beach Motor Inn" in gold italics. You still have the card. You saw it when you were looking for your old bikini to pack for this weekend. The postcard is in your lingerie chest at home, a piece of tape holding it together where you'd torn it in half. You don't remember why. It sits there with the lace teddies, and the thongs, and the old diaphragm, and the expired box of condoms. Just part of the scrapbook of useless items that the drawer has become.

You take stock of the lingerie you're wearing tonight. Black plunge bra. High-cut matching panties. Acceptable, but more department store than trendy. When had you stopped buying designer lace and started buying Walmart?

For the last month—almost daily—you had pictured this re-union with Fran. Tanning at the beach. Munching Grotto pizza. Drinking and dancing at The Starboard. Scoring some guys. Playing them like you did fourteen years ago, a game that Fran termed "reckless" when you mentioned it to her during dinner a few hours ago.

You remember how Fran had given you hell that night of senior week when you left The Starboard to walk the beach with the cute fisherman who'd been buying you Fuzzy Navels all evening. (You actually drank Fuzzy Navels then.) You remember accusing Fran of just being jealous because she hadn't scored that night. The next morning, the two of you would make up. She swears that she was only trying to be protective; you main-tain that you were only trying to be your own person. It was the moment when you drew the line of demarcation between the security of sorority walls and the unknowns of post-graduate life.

You wonder whether Fran is still in the motel room or if she's driven into downtown Rehoboth looking for a piano bar and a glass of wine. That's how you picture her now. You can see her sitting alone at a table, leaning back into the curve of the chair, her legs crossed, and her right hand displaying the wine glass in the air as if it contained liquid rubies. She'd be dressed in classic summer style. Probably a Lilly Pulitzer sundress and Newport Wedge sandals. You think of how she looks like her mother—how her clothing is coordinated to the nines, how she wears her blond braid tied with grosgrain ribbon.

You think of that afternoon at the beach, you in the bikini you hadn't worn since before you got pregnant, and Fran in a one-piece Tommy Bahama. You on a beach towel, and Fran under an umbrella. You read the signs: the connection was missing. It was like you and Fran were on different vacations together. It was like you were at the beach with Mrs. Whooton. She looked at you over her Maui Jim sunglasses. She looked like a freakin' *Vogue* cover. She told you she's engaged—finally—and she wanted to tell you here in Dewey.

Engaged?

Yes, she's engaged, and her fiancé is a VP of something or other. You no longer have the card to trump her mother's hand. Once again, Fran has it all: the looks, the money, the success, and the guy. Just like in college. Fran was invited to pledge the Delta Gammas before you. Fran's parents took her to Europe every summer and invited you to tag along as her guest. Fran lived the dream that the two of you had envisioned that afternoon when you were painting fingernails and giggling about meeting the right men, about marrying, about making your careers.

"I want you to be my matron of honor, of course."

Matron of honor. *Matron*? The word stops you. You cringe.

Beach boy thinks you're chilly. He puts his arm around you. He blames the air conditioner nearest the bar. He suggests you and he leave and take a walk on the beach. "We can look at the ocean," he purrs. He runs the side of his left hand along your thigh, and it seems so obvious, but feels so sexy. He pulls you closer, between his knees on the barstool. He kisses your mouth. You taste the warmth of the whiskey on his lips and inhale the fragrance of his skin, the hot smell of musk and sweat. The scent touches some ancient part of your memory. You think, "Screw her and her wedding plans. Screw her and her Delta Gamma pink fingernails." In your mind, you substitute "look at the ocean" with "screw," and tell beach boy that you'd "love to."

He guides you down Saulsbury Road. The heat you feel isn't diminished by the ocean breeze. Neither of you talk. You let him lead the way. You're committed to doing this. No turning back now. Still, you wonder if your underwear is pretty enough and if the night is dark enough to hide your body's flaws. Your chest flutters as you wonder whether he has a condom with him. You wish you'd been smart enough to have taken care of this yourself. Did you learn nothing from the last time you walked this beach with a guy, the fisherman, fourteen years ago? You should have packed a condom in your purse just in case, but you didn't know that you really would do more than flirt at The Starboard tonight.

Beach boy stops near a lifeguard chair. You figure that it might be the one where he sits during the day. He leans you against the wood frame and gives you a passionate kiss, pushing his body tightly against yours, letting you know that he's ready for you. You feel a rush of excitement, but feel crazy scared at the same time.

Your mind flashes to a wedding. Fran in a Carolyn Herrera gown. Flowers everywhere. Fran's dad walking her down the aisle. *Your* dad didn't walk *you* down an aisle. Your parents couldn't bear the thought of a wedding where you would have to wobble past their family and friends in a gown meant to camouflage the "bun in the oven." Instead, your dad gave Jack directions to the justice of the peace and a warning that he'd better provide for you, and treat you well, and raise the child you and he had made that night on the beach. Max.

Before anything really begins, just as beach boy starts to run his hand under the bottom hem of your dress, everything falls apart. The game. The plan. You push him away and dissolve, tears pouring out, even though you know the timing is bad. You know that the tears aren't about Fran's golden life. The tears are for *yourself.* For how easily you could have broken a vow. For how much you could have hurt your son or ended your marriage. How cheaply you were willing to give up your honor. And for what? To relive a magical night from a senior week so long ago, in hopes of finding what you thought you'd lost—your sexuality?

It confuses beach boy. "What's wrong?" he asks.

You tell him that you've walked this beach before. You tell him that you made a baby. You tell him about Max and Jack and your marriage. The words spill out.

Beach boy changes his approach. He says it's okay, holds your chin in his hand the way he's probably seen in some made-for-television movie on the Hallmark channel. He invites you back to his place, where he promises to make everything all better. You get the vibe that he's done this before, that you're not his first cougar, nor will you be his last. You feel like a fool. For over a month, you dreamed of this night and how it would make you feel. You were wrong. So, you say, "The fault, Dear Brutus, is not in our stars but in ourselves."

He looks confused. It doesn't compute. Why would it? Who quotes Shakespeare on the beach in Dewey where they'd gone to get laid?

"My name's Andy," he says.

You say, "It doesn't matter."

Beach boy may not have read *Julius Caesar,* but he's smart enough to realize that he's not getting any tonight, and that he's wasted three Tanqueray and tonics on you. Suddenly, you've become just another loony bitch to him. He mutters "nut case" and heads back toward The Starboard. He'll score before the last call tonight. Probably the busty cheerleader, if she hasn't already gone off with her second choice.

But it doesn't sting. It doesn't matter. *He* doesn't matter. He probably feels played, and you guess that he's not used to being played, especially by a cougar he'd found sitting alone at the bar and thought would be an easy catch.

You walk away like you could have when you were twenty-one. Except that, if you had, then there wouldn't be a Max, and you would never have known that tiny little baby's entrance into the world, or the joys of potty training, or Little League, or his hugs for Mommy. And deep down, you know that Jack loves you. And really, you love him, too. It's just been a bit of a bad patch, that's all. Blame it on Fran's Christmas card. Blame it on second guesses. Blame it on your cancer scare. Just a scare, but it was enough for you to want to turn back time and start over.

Ring Fran's cell phone. Call her Frenchie, an old nickname from your sorority days. Ask her if she'd like some pizza with an old friend to celebrate her upcoming nuptials. While you wait outside Grotto Pizza for her, phone Jack and tell him you're having a good time. Laugh when he asks if you went to The Starboard and then say, "Wish you were here." Only this time, you really mean it.

That Kind of Girl

Surprisingly, the cottage is exactly as Dana, our coworker, had described it—a yellow-shingled house with intense blue wooden shutters and a wide front porch with a small balcony above it—a classic Bethany Beach cottage, and less than two blocks from the boardwalk. Usually, Dana embellishes everything beyond recognition, but this time, her description of the perfect summer cottage was accurate.

Laney and I, exhausted from a rough week at work and a long drive from DC, can't wait to unpack and start our well-deserved vacation.

"Lucky Dana to own a beach house," Laney says. "I don't even own a decent car."

"But remember," I tell her, "The house is an investment, a rental property." I hand her suitcase to her. "I wonder if she has to give half of the rent to her ex."

Laney grins. "Nah. Ricky is out of the picture. She got the cottage in their settlement." She takes a key from her work lanyard and holds it in the air like a victory torch. "Vacation at last!"

"She only gave us one key?" I hadn't paid attention during the passing of the key at the office today, ridiculous as it sounds. I was so anxious to leave DC before 3 p.m. to beat the Bay Bridge traffic that my mind had been focused only on escaping quickly.

Laney shrugs. "Dana probably has an extra one hidden under the mat on the porch."

Sometimes I wonder how Laney keeps her job at the Delaney & Smith law firm. She is light years from being a rocket scientist. "No one keeps a spare key under a mat anymore," I tell her.

She lifts the mat anyway and seems genuinely surprised that there's only sand and a few dead bugs under it. "There's probably an extra key hanging up inside the hallway. That's where my parents always keep their spare." Again, she shrugs her shoulders, a habitual gesture that she uses whenever she's confused. The guys at work think it's cute; I think it makes her look like a Disney character Pez dispenser. Definitely Ariel with her long red hair. She puts the key into the door lock and twists it. "That's weird. It's already unlocked. I'll bet keys just aren't used in these beach towns and that's why she only gave us this one. There's probably no crime down here except for a drunk driver or two."

The coffee I'd been gulping during the stressful drive begins to churn in my stomach. Maybe I watch too many episodes of CSI, but this unlocked door gives me a queasy feeling. Or perhaps it's just the bag of kettle chips we devoured on the way from DC.

Inside the cottage, things get stranger. There are two empty beer bottles and some crumpled McDonald's bags on the coffee table. Wet towels hang over the banister of the staircase, and music is coming from the second floor. Laney and I stand in the entranceway, holding tight to our suitcases, weighing whether to proceed or run like hell, which is usually what I scream at the TV whenever I watch a horror movie. But with the afternoon sun filling the room, it's hard to believe that we could be in any real danger.

I pull out the directions Dana gave us and double-check the address. We're in the right place. "Maybe we should call Dana," I whisper.

Laney shakes her head. "Cece, we have a signed contract for

this entire week, Friday to Friday. This house is ours, contracted and paid." Okay, so maybe Laney actually has an inkling of contract law; maybe some of it rubbed off on her fingers as she passed the paperwork to her boss. Another shrug. "Maybe some renters from last week have overstayed their time. That would explain the missing second key."

"But Dana didn't mention anything about other renters, and she certainly wouldn't have overlapped rental agreements. She's too smart for that."

"Maybe she forgot. Everybody knows that Mr. Delaney has been running her into the ground lately to make up for the time she missed during her divorce proceedings."

The radio shuts off, and we hear the sound of footsteps on the wood floor of the upper hallway. My feet want to run, but before I can grab Laney to rush out the door, a guy with a towel wrapped around his waist comes sprinting down the steps, clearly unaware of our presence.

"Oh, God!" he says when he sees us. He pushes back his damp wavy black hair. "I didn't know anyone was down here." Then he calls out, "Zach? What's going on here?" No answer. "Did Zach invite you or something? Are you the girls from the Rusty Rudder last night?"

"I don't know any Zach, and I've never been to the Rusty Rudder," I say, letting my bags drop to the floor. "Who are you and why are you in our rental?"

"*Your* rental? No way. Zach and I have this place until Sunday afternoon."

"I don't know who let you think that. Laney and I rented this cottage from the owner, Dana Connelly. Friday to Friday. That makes it ours, starting today."

The guy rolls his eyes. "Dana? Drama Queen Dana? She has no right to rent out this cottage. It isn't hers. It belongs to Ricky. They got a divorce, you know."

I dig into my purse for our copy of the rental agreement. "Yes, we know they got a divorce." His name-calling irritates me. Sure, Dana can be a bit dramatic, but she's our friend, and I intend to defend her. "Dana is a friend of ours. We've heard every detail of the legal stuff between her and … (to drive home the point, I make up a name) Rat's Ass Ricky." Even as I say the name, I know it sounds stupid and I doubt that this guy is going to buy it.

Laney jumps in with, "And we know for a fact that Dana got the cottage in the divorce decree. So it's, uh, Rat's Ass Ricky that doesn't have the right to rent it to anyone."

If looks can be sarcastic, the expression on the face of the guy in the towel exudes it. "Really? You know it for a fact? Well, Rat's Ass Ricky has our money, and we have his signature on our rental contract, which is a Sunday-to-Sunday agreement, so we've got two more days. Since possession is nine-tenths of the law, I guess you're going to have to find a hotel room until then." Then he adds, "That is, unless Rat's Ass Ricky rented it to someone after us, in which case, you're going to need that hotel room a bit longer." He holds open the door to usher us out.

I wave our rental contract at him, pointing to the dates. "Our week starts today. We're not leaving."

The guy raises an eyebrow. "Oh yeah? That might be awkward. I plan to watch tennis. The US Open is on the sports channel …"

"And?"

"I prefer to watch TV naked." He lets the door slam shut.

I have a keen sense of when someone is bluffing. "Go for it," I dare.

He drops his towel, and Laney squeals, "Omigod!" Considering where she's staring, I'm not sure if her exclamation is a reaction to his dropping the towel, or if it's an assessment of his exposed anatomy. Not that I am looking *there*, of course. That's what his little show is all about—trying to freak us out. It's not going to work on me. I lock my stare to his face.

Okay, so sometimes I'm wrong about bluffers. I pretend not to care, and I give him my best smart-ass smile. "We'll just call Dana to clear this up." But my smile disappears when I discover that my cell phone is dead. I'd forgotten to recharge it in the car after a long day of using it at work. Quickly changing tactics, I say, "Better yet, Laney, you call Dana. You have her number on speed dial, right?" I ask, trying to send a silent communication to Laney that she should go along with my request without questions.

No such luck. Laney is still gawking at the naked guy. "You have it on speed dial, too, Cece."

I shove my dead cell phone screen in front of her face to break her stare. "Laney?"

A bit late, she notices my glare; it's the look I give her at work whenever she's ready to say too much to Mr. Delaney at the morning meetings. "OK. Sure. I'll. Call. Dana," she says as though speaking code.

As Laney digs out her own cell phone, the guy strolls over to the fridge like a participant in a nudist colony parade, takes out a bottle of beer, pops off its cap, and settles onto the sofa with the TV remote in hand.

After several minutes of waiting, and Laney's soft chant of "Answer the phone, Dana; answer the phone, darn it; please answer the damn phone;" it's obvious that Dana is not going to answer.

Suddenly, the door opens behind us and someone whistles, causing Laney and me to jump in surprise.

A quick turn puts me face-to-face with a guy whose looks and body could make him a Hugh Jackman lookalike. I love Hugh Jackman as Wolverine. So sexy. I struggle to put aside these thoughts and put on my business persona. "You must be Zach,"

I say and extend my hand as though greeting a colleague I don't really want to know.

"So Kyle told you all about me?" When he sees that his friend is naked, Zach grins. "Cool! Let's get the party started."

Not leaving the couch, the naked guy who now has a name says, "Don't get so excited, Zach. They're leaving."

"Why?" Zach asks. "How did we get them in the first place?"

"Drama Queen Dana thought she could rent this place to her friends."

"So?"

"So? She doesn't have the right to rent out this cottage, and we still have two days here." Kyle jumps up from the couch, saying, "Screw it, I'm calling Ricky." He bounds up the staircase, making it difficult for me not to notice his muscular butt. If the front is as good as the back, I can understand Laney's "omigod." Not that I'm the least bit interested in him. Kyle is a jerk. If I'm going to fantasize about anyone, it would be Zach, the Hugh Jackman lookalike.

I pull my focus off the topic of hot guys. Laney and I have a whole week to meet better guys than these, guys who would be more gallant than these two barhoppers. Besides, I've got a case to win. Zach and Kyle need to relinquish the cottage to us as specified in our very legal rental contract.

Zach takes a cell phone from his pocket, and I expect him to dial Ricky, but he laughs instead. "Somebody's forgotten something. Kyle let me borrow his phone when I lost mine last night in Dewey."

"At the Rusty Rudder?" I wonder aloud, piecing together what Kyle had said earlier.

"Yeah. Been there?"

"No, but I've heard of it." From your obnoxious buddy, I'd like to add, but I don't.

While Kyle is upstairs passing time with the charade of calling Ricky, Laney jumps into her bubbly Pretty Girl Seeks Hot Guy personality, creating bar chat at the worst possible time. I take control and tell Zach the details of how we arrived with a key and a rental agreement from Dana. He shrugs. Laney giggles. Is it possible that Zach is Laney's perfect match? I'd laugh except that Zach and his buddy are our vacation rental enemies. "So, Laney and I will go get some lunch. When we get back, you and Kyle need to be packing up, okay?"

Laney gives me an are-you-out-of-your-mind glare that softens when Zach offers his solution to the dilemma. "So we only overlap for two days. Big deal. We're grown-ups. How about if we share the cottage for those days? It won't be any different than staying in a dorm. There are three bedrooms upstairs. I have the front bedroom—lucky coin-flip on my part—and Kyle has the one in the back. So, the middle one's up for grabs. You two don't mind sharing that one, right?" His grin tells me that he's imagining girl-on-girl action. That makes it easier for me to dislike him. Hugh Jackman would never behave like this.

Before I can set Zach straight on the matter of the middle bedroom, Kyle returns, but this time his hair is dry and he's wearing clothing: cargo shorts and a "Life Is Simple" T-shirt. Ironic, huh? Not knowing that we're privy to his phone's whereabouts, he says to Laney and me, "Ricky said to call the police if you girls won't leave. The divorce paperwork gave him sole ownership of this cottage."

Zach holds up Kyle's missing cell phone, "Buddy, you're busted."

I say, "Payback's a bitch."

"Come on, Kyle. We can't just toss them out," Zach says to him. "Like I said to the girls, we're adults. We can share for two days."

Kyle looks ready to protest, and for once, I am in complete agreement with him. We both start to speak at the same time, and our words jumble over one another, mixing together. "Let them go ... Really it isn't ... to a hotel ... fair since we ... for two days ... paid for the whole week."

But Zach grabs our suitcases from the floor and starts up the stairs. "You girls can have my half of the cottage."

Laney, who's following him as though he's our bellhop, turns on the stairs to wink at me, which just infuriates me all the more. I'd ask if she was so stupid or so sleazy to take Zach's offer, but that would be rhetorical. Yes to both of those questions. I've never seen Laney leave a Friday afternoon happy hour alone, which is just another reason why accepting the invitation to share a bedroom with her would be like going back to the University of Maryland, where I spent too many nights crashing on someone else's floor while my roommate Shari did the dirty deed in our dorm room.

Kyle stomps out the front door like a spoiled child, leaving the US Open tennis balls thwacking in the background, and I'm stuck in limbo, unable to make a phone call to Dana and unwilling to follow my suitcase up the stairs.

The car keys in my hand offer a solution—a place to think and a chance to recharge my cell phone. Despite being tired from the long drive here, I expect that a casual drive up Route 1 with its view of the dunes and the Indian River Bay will relax me. Wrong! How can I not have realized that Laney and I are not the only vacationers escaping to the beach in August? I feel as though my car is stuck on a bumper-to-bumper conveyor belt and is moving north with no assistance from me. The sign for Dewey Beach reminds me of the scattered details of Zach and Kyle's escapades at the bars last night, and I start to worry about having left my air-headed coworker alone in the beach house with one of them. Whatever relaxation I had expected to get from this drive is gone. Duty demands that I get back to the beach house to save Laney, though I don't know if I'm saving her from Zach or from herself.

With the car barely turned off and me still sitting in the driver's seat, I hear Laney's squeaky giggle and see her emerge from the house with Zach, both of them in bathing suits. She tosses her house key through my opened sunroof. "Hey, girl! Zach and I are hitting the beach to watch the sunset. See ya!" And off they go, hand-in-hand, like a couple. Seriously? They just met!

"Isn't it a bit late in the day?" I call to them even though they're already crossing Atlantic Avenue and are less than a block from the boardwalk and beach.

Why was I so worried that Zach would take advantage of her? She seems perfectly at ease with my Hugh Jackman. Damn it. Once again, Laney gets the guy, and, like a fickle witness in court, she jumps to the other side and loses my case. Thanks! I slam the front door to release my need to punch Laney.

The TV is broadcasting the tennis match to an empty living room. Good. Kyle is still out, and I have the whole beach house to myself. A quick tour gives me the layout, and I end my exploration in the bedroom that I seem to be sharing with Laney. Yep. Laney is as sloppy with her unpacking as she is with the general appearance of her desk at work. Her suitcase looks like Fourth of July fireworks exploded its contents all over the bed.

The bed? There's only one bed in this room? No way! I refuse to share a bed with Laney. How could she have thought this would be okay with me? It's time to weigh my options: I could get a hotel room, or I could just drive back home to DC and leave her here in Bethany. A hotel room will push my Visa card close to the max and, worse, would let Kyle win. That's not going to happen. The other option of leaving Laney stuck in coastal Delaware with two strangers is just as bad. Even if she deserves it. Damn! Zach wins. Well, better Zach than Kyle.

Then I notice the wooden frame with tiny wheels under the bed. A roll-out trundle bed. I sweep her stuff off the top part of the bed and onto this moveable one. "Surprise, Laney!" I tug the trundle bed with its pile of Laney's stuff to the other side of the room and begin the task of claiming my territory, like setting boundaries on the first day of freshman dorm. I carefully unpack my own things, neatly arranging the items on my side of the room, finishing by placing my folded PJs on top the pillow of the bed to make clear to Laney that she may have accepted the cottage deal, but I get to choose the bed. Amazingly, I don't feel childish about this at all.

Next, I check the bedroom door for a working lock. Good, there's a deadbolt. Not that a door isn't breakable. Of course, the guys didn't strike me as being evil or dangerous; they're just annoying and rude. And, with Laney's permission, they're wrecking the start of my vacation. I may have to share a cottage for two days, but I won't play nice with them, not even with Laney, now that she's a traitor.

I hear the door downstairs open and close, so I echo it by slamming the bedroom door. Whoever returned—Kyle, Zach, and/or Laney—deserves my anger. When the TV gets louder, I know who returned. Now what? Battle Kyle for the remote control as the first step in making the last two days of his vacation as miserable as he's making the first two days of mine? I feel a headache coming on. I've got to get out of here. Maybe a walk around town would lighten things up for me. I put on my bathing suit and cover it with a wrap skirt and my "Let the Sun Shine" T-shirt to be ready for anything since, so far, this trip to Bethany has been surprise after surprise.

When I go downstairs, Kyle doesn't move his eyes from the television, though I know that he notices me because he mutters, "bitch," under his breath, yet loud enough to be sure that I hear him.

I mutter back, "asshole," and leave the cottage.

The walk is just what I need. Bethany Beach is such a cute

little town, very much still holding on to the old-beach-town appearance. It reminds me of the summer trips of my childhood to the old Ocean City with Aunt Fern. Most of the newer beach cottages mimic the designs of the mid-20th century, and many of the shops are original to that time. Of course, shopping lifts my spirits a bit, as it always does, and I have four bags of new summer shirts and handcrafted jewelry before my stomach demands food. The sun is setting over the ocean as I enjoy a Caesar salad at Mango's and unwind with a piña colada served, to my delight, in a souvenir ceramic coconut that will make a cute pencil holder for my desk at work.

Unlike Laney, I'm a lightweight when it comes to alcohol, so my walk back to the cottage feels wobbly, as I focus on holding tight to my shopping bags and not dropping the now-empty ceramic coconut. At the cottage, everything is as I expect: The front door is unlocked, the TV is running the seemingly endless tennis competition, Kyle is doing his imitation of Jabba the Hutt on the sofa, and Laney and Zach are MIA. When I take the first step of the staircase, Kyle says, "They came back, changed clothes, and went off to Dewey with my car. And my cell phone, which Zach better not lose if he wants to live to see another day."

When I turn back to toss off a smart reply, I lose my balance and fall face forward to the floor.

Kyle rushes over to me. "Are you okay?"

I push myself up to a sitting position. Knowing that my fall was less than graceful, I feel embarrassed, though I try to hide this. "The shopping bags broke my fall." I hold up the coconut cup that is still safely in the grasp of my right hand. "Safe and sound."

"And drunk," Kyle says.

He couldn't just laugh with me? It was funny, right? He had to state the obvious—a shitty thing to do, though I should have expected that from him. "I am not! Besides ..." I point my cup toward the increased number of empty beer bottles on the coffee table, "you've had way more than I have."

"Yes, but apparently I can hold my drinks better than you."

The gauntlet has been thrown. I manage to stand up on my own, hang my purse on the banister, kick my shopping bags out of the way, and lift my coconut in a salute. "Challenge accepted."

When Kyle laughs at me, my determination soars. I walk to the sofa in what must look like the walk-the-line test given to drunk drivers, and I plop down on the overstuffed cushions. Kyle opens two more bottles of beer from the counter fridge and joins me. "Are you sure?" he asks. "These are craft beers. They have a higher proof than regular beer." He holds a bottle to me, pointing to the fish logo and a beer name written in French.

I have no idea what a craft beer is, any more than I know what the label says. Even if I weren't a bit drunk, I doubt that my high school French would have helped me translate its name. Very few French words remain in my vocabulary; it was never my … forté. "How do you know what I've had? Maybe I drink craft beer all the time." I hold out the coconut.

"That's not exactly the type of glass used for serving Belgian ale," he says. His grin tells me that he thinks that's funny.

"And I guess your drinking it directly from the bottle is classy?"

I win. He pours the dark beer into the coconut.

"Cheers!" I say. I take a large gulp and try to hide my surprise at a taste that seems more like liquid raisins than like any beer I've ever had. Okay, so he's right; I've never had a beer like this, but I'll never let him know that. I mirror his smart grin. "Can't you find a good American beer?"

"It is an American beer."

"But you said it's Belgian ale."

"Belgian ale is a type of beer, not its place of origin." He says it with the same condescending tone as my seventh grade history teacher telling us how stupid our test answers were.

Crap! I don't know anything about beer, but I will not let him know about my lack of beer education. I roll my eyes in fake annoyance. "I was only testing you," I say. "And don't give me that look." Another sip. I move the beer around in my mouth in the way I've seen wine connoisseurs on television do when they rate wines.

Kyle seems to find this amusing. "Go ahead. Describe the taste."

I take a few more sips, stalling for time. Finally, I say, "You bought the beer. If you're so knowledgeable about it, how would you describe the taste?"

He takes a sip and stares at his bottle. "A deep mahogany ale, brewed with Belgian beet sugars, green raisins, and a sense of purpose," he says.

His description stops me. How can such a jerk be so eloquent? I blurt out, "That's so poetic," and actually mean it.

He points to the label and grins. "I'm just reading what the brewery says about it."

I can't tell if my blush is embarrassment or alcohol, but I know that I'm not steady enough to march out of the room with any dramatic flair, so I ignore his quip and continue sipping the tasty beer. Since he's still staring at me and waiting for my response, I say, "I did taste the raisins. I just didn't know about the beets."

"And you like it," he says rather than asks.

I chug the rest of the beer in my coconut and hold out the empty container to him. "Sure. Why not?"

"You've had enough alcohol."

"When did you become my parents? If you don't want to give me another one of your beers, I'll just have to find a liquor store and get some of my own," I say, glancing around for my purse with the car keys in it, and suddenly not sure if I brought it home from the restaurant. "Omigod, where's my purse?"

Kyle points toward the staircase where I had left my purse dangling from the end of the banister. "But you're not driving until you're sober."

"Then I guess I'll have to stick with your beer stash," I say, and weave my way to the counter fridge. "Do you want another one?" I ask him

"No, I'd better stop ... just in case."

"Just in case?"

"In case I have to drive your car for you."

I may be woozy, but I know how to give attitude. I carry two bottles of beer to the sofa and plop one down in front of him. "I don't need a chaperone." I should have said designated driver, but I couldn't remember the term in time. When I try to unscrew the top of my bottle, it won't move, even when I wrap the edge of my T-shirt around it.

He laughs. "But you do need a bottle opener."

Undeterred, though doubting how much longer I can stay upright, I slowly walk back to the counter, hold the bottle opener in the air for Kyle's attention, and suddenly I'm overcome by a rush of nausea. I toss the opener in his general direction and prepare to rush upstairs to the bathroom. But when I turn toward the staircase, my dinner, my piña colada, and the beer will hold down no longer. I rush out the front door and vomit into the bushes. Omigod. I've vomited in front of him. It's degrading. It's ... Then the tears come.

Kyle holds open the screen door. "Don't worry about it. Come back inside and sit down."

I'm so embarrassed. This is something I'd expect of Laney, but not of me. I know that I'm a one-drink woman; that's all I ever have to drink during happy hour in DC. Why in the world did I do this to myself?

I manage to get to the bottom step of the staircase. I feel safe here, halfway between the front door and my bedroom, and on a wooden floor without rugs in case I have another mishap.

Kyle disappears from the room for a moment and returns with a wad of dampened paper towels. He puts one on the back of my neck and wipes my mouth with another. Then he sits next to me. "It's okay, Cece. It happens to all of us." With another towel, he gently wipes my face, and I don't object. The coolness of the dampened towel feels great. His taking care of me feels even better.

"You know my name," I manage to say.

"Laney mentioned it on her way out the door with Zach. She asked me to tell you where she went."

"Even drunk, I could've figured that out myself," I say. "Laney and I should have gone to a hotel. Now that she's latched onto Zach, the whole vacation will be about him."

"Laney's not much of a friend, is she? Not that Zach is much of one either."

"They do belong together. Pez dispensers," I tell him. He looks at me strangely, so I do the shoulder shrug. "Pez dispensers. I thought Laney was an original until I saw Zach do the stupid shrug, too."

Zach howls with laughter. "Pez dispenser. I never thought of that." He imitates Zach's shrug. "Hey, dude, I don't know where my cell phone is."

I join in with my impersonation of Laney. Shrug. "Maybe there's a key beneath the door mat," I say and then add a high-pitched giggle. But the laughter just turns my stomach more, and I am afraid that I might vomit again. "Maybe I should go upstairs and lie down."

"I'll help you up the stairs, in case you get dizzy."

A car door slams, and Zach and Laney enter the cottage kissing and groping one another as though Kyle and I aren't there. Zach tosses car keys to his buddy, and says, "Hey, don't wake us up early. And if you hear sounds coming from the front bedroom, don't be knocking at the door; just be jealous."

Laney shrugs at me and giggles. Then Zach grabs her butt, and she squeals and runs between Kyle and me, up the stairs with Zach pursuing. A bedroom door slams.

"That better not be my room," I say.

"Not Zach's style. He prefers his own bed."

"Laney won't care." I think of all the times that Laney left the DC bars with someone new, and how I worried that something bad could happen to her as she went off to God-knows-where.

"You and Laney are so different." Kyle says. "She's more like Dana."

I nod. "Laney's a party girl, but a nice party girl."

"I didn't know there was any such thing as a nice party girl. Easy maybe, but not nice."

I want to tell him that he's wrong, but how do I explain that someone can be a bit wild but also be a good person at heart? "She was nice to me when I got my job at Delaney & Smith. While the other paralegals were busy kissing up to the partners, she went out of her way to help me get on my feet there."

"So you owe her?"

"It's more than that. We have each other's back. How about you and Zach?"

"We were frat brothers in college. We had some good times there. He's still fun to be with ... until he hooks up with a girl. Then he becomes obsessed for a night or two, maybe more if she's really hot, and he dumps his friends until he gets bored with the girl."

"And he's still your friend?" I ask.

"Minus the girl fault, Zach is a good guy, too. He's loyal to his bro's ..."

"But not to his ho's," you finish his sentence. "How long do you think he'll give Laney?"

"Until Sunday night, probably," Kyle says. "He'll get her phone number, but he won't call her. Will Laney be crushed over it?"

I shake my head. "No, she'll move on, too."

Kyle nods. "They deserve each other." Then he says, "I'm glad that he didn't hook up with you."

That gets my attention. "Really? Why?"

A loud squeal from the front bedroom momentarily interrupts us.

"Why are you glad that Zach and I didn't hook up?" I repeat.

"You're not that kind of girl."

"What kind of girl am I?" I ask him.

He smiles, but doesn't answer my question. "You're not going to get any sleep in a bedroom next to them. We should trade. You should take my bedroom in the back of the house. It might be far enough away to give you some quiet."

Why didn't he answer my question? "No, I'll be fine," I say and climb the steps alone, using the railing to steady myself.

"Cece," he calls to me.

I stop and wait for him to tell me what kind of girl I am, but instead he says, "I'm sorry about the whole naked tennis thing this afternoon. I was being an asshole. Just like you said."

"It's okay. I was a bit of a bitch myself."

Safely inside my room, I kick the trundle bed that Laney will never need to sleep on now that she's with Zach. I grab the wall to keep from falling over as I rub my sore toes. Then, I slip into my PJs and let myself fall across the bed, but I know I won't sleep. I saw a different Kyle tonight. A side that I really like. His concern when I fell. His gentleness when he wiped my face. His offer to trade rooms. My mind keeps running on about him. My brain keeps asking, why didn't he answer my question?

I need to shut down my mind. I need to sleep off the drinks. But, of course, that's not going to happen tonight. The sounds coming from Zach's bedroom are like audio porn. I pull the pillow over my head and wish I had earplugs. Kyle was right; I should have accepted his offer to trade rooms.

I'm such an idiot. I totally misjudged Kyle. It's always the same with me. I go into defense mode and get competitive. At happy hour, while Laney's flirting and having a great time, I'm always arguing politics with whichever poor guy got stuck with me. She leaves arm-in-arm with someone, and I leave alone.

The noise from Zach and Laney crescendos. I can't stay here. It makes me feel embarrassed. And dirty. And my head is starting to hurt again. If I'm going to avoid a hangover, I'd better get hydrated. I think I can handle the walk to the kitchen.

The hallway is dark except for the thin light that comes through the window from the street lamp outside. I see that Kyle's bedroom door is closed, and I guess that he went to bed, too. I want to knock on his door and ask the question again. "What kind of girl am I?"

Downstairs, I notice dim light in the living room and hear the now-muted television. Kyle is stretched out on the sofa half-watching Jimmy Fallon on the *Tonight Show*. I lean against the stair rail and gaze at him.

Kyle becomes aware of me, and without my asking, he says, "You're the kind of girl who's more than a one-night stand. You're the kind of girl who has substance. You're the kind of girl that a guy marries."

He motions, and I go to him. His arms reach out and I nestle into them. Cuddling on the sofa with Kyle feels more right than I ever would have thought. I sigh and let go of all the day's junk.

"I'm sorry about this rental mess," he whispers.

"Don't be," I tell him. "It isn't your fault. Dana and Ricky are to blame." A loud headboard bang echoes down the staircase, and I add, "Besides, Laney and Zach got what they both wanted."

"How about you?" he asks. "Are you still upset about this arrangement?"

"Not anymore," I tell him.

Kyle kisses my forehead and says, "Me, either. I've got what I want."

I lean into him and know that I did, too.

Dancing at the Legion

"I just can't."

"Sure you can," Babs insists, holding up a bright red calico circle skirt. "It'll fit you just right. A little dancing and you'll need a size smaller."

She's probably right. She looks great, especially at our age. It must be all the activities she does. Babs was always a joiner, even when I first met her at Kenwood High School in 1965. It was Babs who convinced me to try out for cheerleading, and Babs who dragged me to auditions for the school musicals, and Babs who introduced me to Gary, the man I married right out of high school and loved for close to forty-five years. And still love. Death doesn't stop love.

"It's time you kick up your heels, Dottie."

Babs is the only person, other than Gary, who was allowed to call me that name. Everyone else calls me Dorothy. Sure, it sounds formal and old-fashioned, but that suits me just fine. I was named after my favorite aunt, and keeping her name is a way of honoring her.

"Are you listening, Dottie?"

It snaps me out of my memories and back to earth. "Yes, yes."

"No, no," she answers back. "If you were listening, you would have answered my question." She holds up a denim circle skirt. "You can wear this one if you really don't like the red skirt. If you want to be boring, that is. Personally, I think the red puts you into the right frame of mind and brings out the cheerleader in you."

"Cheerleader? Those days are long gone."

"Maybe for you," Babs says. "Not for me." She demonstrates a lunge, with her hands held out as though shaking pom-poms. She makes me laugh, as she always has. "See? You *can* laugh! Dottie, can we talk plainly here? Gary's been gone for over four years, and it's time you start dating again. You'd want the same for him if the situation were reversed."

Would I? Sure. Maybe.

"I'm not saying you have to find another husband. Just have some fun," Babs says. "At our age, it's just good to find companionship with someone of the opposite sex. Someone who appreciates you for the woman that you are, and makes you feel good with a compliment now and then. Someone to give you a reason to splash on a little makeup and comb your hair. Someone to have drinks with, or share some buttered popcorn with at the movies. What's wrong with that?"

I nod. I get it. She's right. I touch the fabric of the denim skirt, and it reminds me of the Levi's jeans I wore in high school. Low-rider jeans that showed off my tiny waist and let me feel the warmth of Gary's arm wrapped around me. "This one." I always liked denim.

"Good!" Babs says, letting go of the hanger. Then she sorts through the blouses in her closet. "This may be a bit more difficult. You've always been bustier than me, so I'll have to lend you one of the stretchier blouses." She pulls out a light-blue paisley shirt with mother-of-pearl snaps. "This one'll look great with the denim." She tosses it across the bed to me. "Thank God we take the same shoe size. Or should I say boot size?" Now she's pulling boxes out from under the bed, peeking under box tops, and declaring, "Not these. Maybe those. Okay, we have a winner!" She tosses a box onto the bed, and its top pops off, revealing a pair of bright-red cowboy boots with two-inch heels.

I gasp, partly by accident, and partly to make a point. "Babs,

I can't even walk—let alone dance—in heels anymore. Foot surgery, remember? I'll wear my tennis shoes, okay?"

"Nope. Not okay." She digs farther, disappearing partway under the bed.

My eyes return to the Western shirt she's chosen for me. Snap closures for my 38Ds? I see a wardrobe malfunction in my future.

"Got it." She wiggles out and hands the box to me.

Inside, I find navy blue boots with flat heels. They're less garish than the red ones, and since Babs is adamant about me dressing the part for this square dance or whatever it is at the American Legion, these blue ones are my best choice. I pull them on and take a few steps. Comfortable. And kind of cute, though I'll never tell Babs that or she'll be dragging me all over Sussex County to fill my own closet with costumes for every occasion: a sequined top for a disco-themed dance, a muumuu for a Hawaiian luau, a Mrs. Santa dress for Christmas parties, and, God forbid, a diaper and wings for Valentine's Day. I have no intention of turning my spare closet into a costume department. It's not like I'll ever go dancing like this when I return home to Baltimore. I just need to go along with Babs' plans for my three-week visit here. I was kind of hoping that the visit would consist mostly of catching a few rays on the deck of her Port Lewes townhouse, watching the ferries dock, and catching up with each other's lives—not going to a dance event and wearing a costume as though it were Halloween rather than a regular summer day.

"Put the rest of it on, Dottie. Come on. I want you to see the whole picture."

I slip out of my sweats and dress the part of the cowgirl. I see my reflection in the full-length mirror on the back of the bedroom door, and for a moment I'm sixteen again and going to the homecoming costume party with Gary, he in overalls and a cowboy hat and me in Western dress with full skirt and embroidered top. We kissed during the hayride.

"You look great, Dottie. Wait 'til Mickey sees you."

Mickey. The name stops me like walking into a wall. "Who's Mickey?"

"One of my friends. There's a bunch of us who hang out together. Like the old days, Dottie. Remember how after the games our crowd went to Gino's for burgers? We practically took over the place. It was fun, right? So, it's the same at the Legion. Our group takes over three tables, usually. Mostly women, and three couples, but we have a few single guys, too."

"And Mickey is your boyfriend?" I ask, hoping that she's not planning on fixing me up with someone. Of course the last time she fixed me up with a guy was in my sophomore year at Kenwood. Gary. My one and only sweetheart since that autumn day in 1966.

"Mickey isn't anybody's boyfriend. He's just one of the guys."

"Babs," I start, but she cuts me off.

"No, I'm not planning a blind date for you. I wouldn't do that. At least not without discussing it with you first. But I hope you'll be friendly at least. Dance if someone asks you. Have some fun."

I think of that phone call from Babs, when she hatched this idea of my coming to the beach and spending time with her, giving us the chance to share more than the seasonal cards and bi-yearly long phone conversations that we've exchanged since her move to coastal Delaware. "Spend all of July," Babs had said to me on the phone. "You're retired. There's nothing to keep you from getting away and trading boring Baltimore for lovely Lewes." This is the first week of visiting with Babs and already I wish that I had only committed to a one-week visit rather than almost a month. I'm barely unpacked, and already she's got me going to a dance at the Legion. Then what? Hitting the local happy hours? Learning to surf? Skinny dipping in the community swimming pool? Babs has always been the more adventurous one, and apparently that hasn't changed with age. The only thing that saved me as a teenager was that I had Gary to rescue me. Now I'm on my own, and confrontation has never been comfortable for me. Not even friendly confrontation.

As I put on some makeup, sharing the bathroom mirror with my old friend, I'm reminded that Babs was always the bedazzle queen. Watching her cake on blue shadow and mascara, I can see that she still is. Yet Babs doesn't look like a tart. She has a real talent with her makeup. And an eye for colors. Me? I dust light-brown shadow over my eyelids, just enough to give some dimension, and an even lighter dash of blush on my cheeks.

Babs looks at me through the mirror surface. "Well that certainly looks dull. You need a bit of a makeover, Dottie, so I'm going to be your makeup artist." And before I can form the words of dissent, she adds, "Trust me."

My brown lids become blue, the dark under-eye circles get brightened, and the years start to drop away. It looks a bit over-the-top for me, but at least it isn't as glaring and shimmering as hers. Babs looks like a cross between high-fashion runway model and drag queen. I couldn't pull off that look. On Babs, it works.

The first thing I notice at the American Legion is the number of smokers sitting at the large rectangular bar and what seems like a choreographed ritual: take a sip of beer, take a puff of cigarette, say something, gesture with the cigarette, laugh, take another sip of beer, and repeat. But before I can say anything to Babs about not wanting to sit at the bar or anywhere near it, I hear calls of, "Hey, Babs! Thought you weren't going to make it," "Hey, Babs, new skirt?" and "Come here, girl, I got a kiss for you." It's like we stepped into the old television show, *Cheers*. I stop walking behind her and watch as she twirls from patron to patron, giving out hugs to the women and quick cheek-kisses to the men.

"You didn't think I'd miss dancing to Banjo Pete and the Callers, did you?" she answers loud enough for the whole bar to hear.

She gets a "Yee-hah!" from the bartender, a young woman with a perky black ponytail and a face that reveals too many days spent at the beach.

Babs waves me over, and I put on a smile, even though my heart is pounding with panic at having to fit in with a group of strangers who also seem to share my friend's loud, outgoing nature. "Everyone, this is my friend Dottie."

No. I draw the line. "My name's Dorothy," I call out to them, surprised by the volume of my own voice.

"Nah," one of the guys says. "You don't look like a Dorothy. Not any more than Babs here looks like a Barbara."

Babs smacks him on the shoulder. "Barbara? I've never been a Barbara. Or a Barbie. Or anything other than Babs."

"Oh yeah?" he says, grabbing her around the waist. "Show me your birth certificate. I'll bet it doesn't say Babs."

My old friend giggles like a schoolgirl and squirms from the guy's arm. "Of course, it doesn't say 'Babs.' It's a piece of paper, Charlie; it can't talk!"

Her friends groan.

"You're just scared to show us your birth certificate because then we'd know your real age, isn't that right?" Charlie says with a smirk.

"I'm younger than you," she answers, and adds, "But then, who isn't?"

Like a stand-up comic, Babs has the crowd howling. The bartender hands her a drink. "Peach whiskey sour, three cherries, and a pink umbrella."

"You're the best, Margie!"

"And what would your friend like?" Margie asks her.

Before I can answer, Babs hands me hers. "Just fix me another. Charlie will bring it to the table for me." She gives Charlie another peck on the cheek. "Won't you, darling?" Then, she whispers something into his ear.

He whistles, and says, "Thirty-three? You don't look a day over thirty-two and a half."

Another of her friends calls out, "Babs, your boots are older than that."

The bar empties into a large hall where the round tables have been grouped around a dance floor with a raised stage at its end. Babs leads me to a center front-row table where the view of the stage is perfect.

The band is finishing its setup, and Babs calls out to one of them, "Hey, Mickey!"

The tallest one of the group looks up and smiles. His full head of silver hair catches the colored lights on the stage. It's obvious he takes good care of himself. No beer belly, and the speaker he's moving doesn't seem heavy to his arms. I figure that he's probably one of those people who jogs every day or goes to a gym to lift weights. This reminds me of how little I've done to keep myself in shape. Being here with Babs brings that point home. I make a mental note to go back to Weight Watchers when I get home and promise myself I'll start using those *Sweating to the Oldies* DVDs again. Babs is right. If I just dropped ten pounds, I'd also drop a dress size and look almost as good as she does. Wearing sweats around the house has hidden the truth from me.

Babs points at me. "Mickey, this is Dottie!"

"Nice to meet you, Dottie!" he calls across the dance floor. "Save me a seat, Babs."

Babs tosses her purse over me and toward the seat to my left. The purse bounces to the floor, and I pick it up and return it to the chair. "So, your friend Mickey is in the band?" I ask.

"No, he's just helping with the setup. Mickey does a lot

around here at the Legion, especially since he lost his wife Ginny to cancer. This is practically his second home. He's a great guy all around."

I'm not sure whether she's telling me this because she has her own eye on him or because she's thinking about setting me up with the guy. A widower for a widow. Well, that's not going to happen. Just because Babs made a great match between Gary and me in high school doesn't mean that I'm willing to try one of her match-ups again.

"You haven't touched that drink, Dottie," she says to me.

"Sure I have," I lie, and take my first sip. Although I was expecting a sour taste, as the name of the drink implied, I'm surprised; the sweet peach liqueur makes it taste like a punch I make for summer afternoons on the back porch.

"Good, right?" She has a know-it-all look on her face that makes me want to fake a sour pucker and refute the drink's deliciousness.

Charlie plops down on the empty seat to the right of Babs and places her drink on the table. "Here you are, princess."

The tables fill up with Babs' boisterous friends from the bar, who chat across the tables in loud voices. I smile and laugh at the jokes, hoping that will be enough participation to get me through this evening. I watch as Babs and Charlie exchange banter like a couple of kids who are "going steady," as everyone used to say when we were in high school. It's fun to watch them. Like viewing a sitcom on the Fox network. This might be a good evening after all. I imagine that Babs will dance the night away with Charlie, and I can just sit here and sip this delicious drink.

Then I remember that the purse on the seat next to me is reserving a place for Mickey. I'll bet Babs is up to something. She can be sneaky that way. She was quite an actress in high school, always getting the role of the smart-talking sidekick in the musicals. She played Ado Annie in *Oklahoma*, and sang the song, "I

Cain't Say No." After the musical was over, that lyric became her signature, and Babs would sing the refrain any time she needed an excuse for doing something daring. Not that she ever needed an excuse.

As though on cue, Mickey approaches the chair and asks, "Is this saved for me?"

He lifts the purse from the chair, and a woman with short salt-and-pepper curly hair calls out, "Mickey! That pink bag isn't right for you at all." The two women next to her laugh.

Mickey holds the purse up against his chest. "Are you sure? I think it brings out the color in my eyes."

The other women eat this up, and it's apparent that they consider Mickey a catch. Good. That lets me off the hook.

Not really. As soon as Mickey sits down, he turns to me with a friendly smile. "Dottie, right?"

"I prefer Dorothy. Babs just won't let go of what she used to call me when we were in high school together."

"So that's where you know her from," he says.

I feel relieved. If Babs didn't tell him about me, then maybe she's not setting us up at all. Anyway, with all the attention he's getting from local females here at the Legion, Mickey certainly doesn't need to be fixed up with a boring visitor like me.

The band starts up, and the lead singer calls out, "Good evening, everyone!"

The crowd enthusiastically returns the greeting with a "Yee-hah."

"Are ya ready for a little Texas two-step?"

The room explodes with responses as couples rush from their tables, among them Babs and Charlie. Two women surround Mickey, and both ask him to dance. He avoids choosing between them by saying, "You know I'm not so good at the two-step."

"Neither is she," the salt-and-pepper woman says, pointing to her friend. "So I guess you'll just have to dance with me. I'm used to leading."

Her friend doesn't seem upset at all. She winks at Mickey and says, "I get the first slow dance then, right?"

The floor is crowded with couples. Some of them glide across the floor, comfortable from years of dancing together. Other couples are same-sex—women who came to the Legion alone or those with husbands who don't like to dance. But everyone seems to be having fun.

The next number called is a line dance, "Boot Scootin' Boogie." Babs stands and says to me, "Just this one, Dottie. Try it. Some kick-ball-changes and a basic grapevine. Like in our high school musicals. Easy. If you hate it, you can stop, and I promise I won't bug you anymore about line dancing. But I think you'll like this." She leads me to the dance floor despite my protests. "And life is too short to sit and watch everyone one else having fun."

The dance is repetitive, and Babs keeps giving me directions like she's my dance tutor, so I pick up the pattern quickly with just an occasional misstep, and nothing devastatingly embarrassing. It's actually kind of fun, like the dances we did in the Sixties, but I don't want to encourage her. So, I smile politely and tell her, "Okay. I danced. Now I get to watch for a while, okay?"

I'm glad that she doesn't act hurt or show her disappointment as I return to my seat.

A slow dance starts up, and Babs announces to me, "Go ahead and sit, wallflower. I've got my man for this dance." She grabs Charlie's hand and says, "Come on, lover boy. They're playing our song."

As I watch them dancing together, I see their faces light up like teenagers at a school dance. Babs has someone *to share some buttered popcorn with at the movies.* Her words hit me like a big dose of reality. She may have given me a mini-makeover this afternoon, but I know that I need a bigger makeover than that.

She's right about me—I am a wallflower. Babs brings happiness and life wherever she goes; what do I bring? Blah. I avoid anything that's new or different. A pang of self-pity shoots through me, and with that, I gulp down the rest of the peach whiskey sour.

"Dorothy?"

I look up and see Mickey standing by my chair.

"Would you like to dance?" he asks.

It's as if he's my knight-in-shining-armor who has come at exactly the right instant to save this damsel-in-distress. Or maybe it's the buzz from the alcohol. Earlier tonight, I would have politely declined, afraid of what dancing with him might mean. But now, I'm ready to *dance if someone asks you*, as Babs had instructed. "Of course," I say. "I'd love to."

Being inside a man's arms and swaying to the music sends goose bumps up my arms. It's like the first time I danced with Gary. I try to stop the feeling, as though I am somehow cheating on my deceased husband, but then, more of Babs' words rush into my mind, *You'd want the same for him if the situation were reversed.*

She was right again. Mind over matter, I relax and let the music and the motion take charge. From across the dance floor, Babs grins and gives a thumbs-up. I laugh and start to reply but then realize that she's signaling Mickey, not me. She did plan this all along. Babs hasn't changed a bit. She maneuvered both Mickey and me into this moment, like arranging chess pieces on a board. Yet for some reason, I don't mind it.

"You're a great dancer," he says to me.

"I must have a great partner."

"Babs says you're in town for a few weeks. Do you think maybe you'd consider going out to dinner with me?"

"Without Babs?" I ask.

He hesitates, and then says, "I guess she can come along, too.

Maybe we can make it a double date." He seems disappointed.

"Oh, I didn't mean that Babs needs to come along. I was just asking if you and I would be dining alone."

"Ah, good. Babs is a great person and a solid friend, but she turns anything into a party. A loud party." Then after a brief pause, he says, "I would rather have a quiet dinner … a date, so you and I can talk and get to know each other better."

"That would be wonderful."

The song ends, and he looks into my eyes. "I should tell you that this will be my first real date since my wife passed, so I might not be any good at it. I probably shouldn't have told you that; it might make you feel weird about going out with me. See, I really am rusty at this dating thing."

"So am I," I tell him. "It'll be my first date, too. So I guess that makes us sixteen years old again."

"We don't need a chaperone, do we?"

"Maybe," I say. "Who knows?"

We walk back to the table where Babs and Charlie are already seated. I lean toward Babs and whisper "You win."

"I know," she says. "I know."

Starry Nights

About the Author

 **Nancy Powichroski Sherman** has been a teacher for over forty years, but a writer since she was old enough to sit at her bedroom window and imagine. She was born and raised in Baltimore, Maryland, where she taught composition, literature, and theatre for thirty-two years in the Baltimore County Public School system. Though retired from this full-time position, she continues her career as an educator teaching an online course she designed for Stevenson University.

When not grading papers, Nancy finds that there are more stories than there are days in a year to write them. Currently, she is juggling several writing projects, including collaborating on a young adult novel that is scheduled for publication in 2015. Her published works include "The Sound of a Tree Falling" and "The Gypsy Heart" (*Delaware Beach Life* magazine) and "Why Your Trashed Vera Wang" and "No Magic Words" (*The Beach House* anthology). She lives in coastal Delaware with her husband Matthew and two Bichon Frises, Pookie and Zoey. Nancy is a member of the Rehoboth Beach Writers' Guild.

Other books by Cat & Mouse Press

The Beach House

What does "beach house" mean to you? Is it a sanctuary, a playground for romance, or a spot for wild escapades? It was these things and more for the twenty-one writers whose stories were chosen for the first book in the Rehoboth Beach Reads series.

The perfect book to tuck in your beach bag or have in your own beach house.
- Susan McAnelly, Browseabout Books

A Rehoboth ABC

From swooping seagulls to frolicking dolphins, the familiar sights and sounds of Rehoboth are captured in this award-winning book for children.

You Know You're in Rehoboth When

How do you know you're in Rehoboth? The dogs are smaller than the martinis, you won't get ketchup with those fries, and happy hour starts at 9 a.m. Whether you are a visitor or a local, you will recognize the unique charm of Rehoboth in this hilarious book.

Purchasing information: www.catandmousepress.com/publications.html

CPSIA information can be obtained at www.ICGtesting.com
Printed in the USA
BVOW04s2112070714

358244BV00006B/31/P